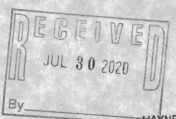

FLYAWAY

FLYAWAY

Kathleen Jennings

A TOM DOHERTY ASSOCIATES BOOK

NEW YORK

FLYAWAY

Copyright © 2020 by Kathleen Jennings

Edited by Ellen Datlow

Interior art by Kathleen Jennings

Designed by Greg Collins

A Tor.com Book
Published by Tom Doherty Associates
120 Broadway
New York, NY 10271

www.tor.com

Tor® is a registered trademark of Macmillan Publishing Group, LLC.

The Library of Congress Cataloging-in-Publication Data is available upon request.

ISBN 978-1-250-26049-9 (hardcover)
ISBN 978-1-250-26048-2 (ebook)

Our books may be purchased in bulk for promotional, educational, or business use. Please contact your local bookseller or the Macmillan Corporate and Premium Sales Department at 1-800-221-7945, extension 5442, or by email at MacmillanSpecialMarkets@macmillan.com.

First Edition: 2020

Printed in the United States of America

0 9 8 7 6 5 4 3 2 1

For Mark and Mary

TABLE OF CONTENTS

FLYAWAY

ALL THAT WAS

Once, somewhere between the Coral Sea and the Indian Ocean but on the way to nowhere, there was a district called—oh, let's call it Inglewell.

Now, of course, it is overlaid by the smooth, sturdy engineering of the mining companies—the towns and their histories have been dug up or made over. A few landmarks remain unchanged: the inevitable memorial to wars long ago and far away, the street names. But almost every town has just such a memorial, and many places have a Spicer Street or a Pinnicke Road. You could never be sure you'd arrived.

But not so long ago it was a cupped palm of country, pinned to time by its three towns: Woodwild, Carter's Crossing, and Runagate, my own.

RUNAGATE—HEART OF INGLEWELL on its stone welcome sign. Thirteen streets, one remaining pub, never a bank. One grocery store with a comfortable bench outside and air-conditioning sighing through the bright plastic strips curtaining the door. A water tower patterned in white and rust and shade. Three churches, each smaller than a house. The clawing precision of hard-won roses planted in wire-fenced gardens on the buried corpses of roadside kangaroos. Geraniums hot as matches. The spice of pepperina, oleander's poison-sapped glow, the hallowed death of angel's trumpets as apricot as sunset. Showgrounds, handsome in dusty cream and pea-green paint; stockyards. A long low school smelling of squashed jam sandwiches, the heady scents of cheap felt-tips and novelty erasers.

Of Inglewell's three towns, only Runagate still had a pulse. Woodwild was already nearly vanished; Carter's Crossing had barely been. They held to each other by fraying ribbons of fractured, blue-black bitumen and cords of ribbed dirt, fringed with pale sand or beaded with blood-red pebbles (not stained by massacres, no, nor cursed, whatever people whispered about how the Spicer family first established Runagate Station).

That triangle tangle of roads and tracks held the district of Inglewell: hills and scrub glittered in the powder-white light, fading to chalk blue; sharp grasses fluttered pale in the paddocks, green and burgundy on the verge; grey huts subsided into themselves like memory. Then the plunge into purple shadows, the troll-rattle of an old timber bridge, a secret of dim emerald and the barrier-shriek of cicadas. Then up again, sky-tumbled, grass-fogged.

It was a fragile beauty: too easy to bleach with dust and history, to dehydrate with heat, rend with the retort of a shotgun or the strike of a bullbar, blind with sun on metal. Easy to turn from it, disgusted and afraid. But if you got out of a car to stretch your legs and instead were still, if you crouched down and waited, it would find you, nosing among the grass like the breeze. The light and loveliness would get into your bones, into your veins. It would beat in your blood like drumming under the ground.

Memory seeped and frayed there, where ghosts stood silent by fenceposts. There the bone horse kept pace with night drivers, while high branches shifted continuously even on breathless days and creaked with the passage of megarrities or other creatures unseen, and at midday long shadows whispered under the trees. And what trees!

Bottle and box, paper and iron, thorned and blossomed under the unutterable light (the sky blue as breath, as enamel, or beaten like copper, everything beneath it turned to metal, or else translucent). Trees like lanterns, like candles, ghosts and bones. The fibrous skeletons of moth-slain cactus and beetle-eaten lantern-bush leaned over the opal-veined bulk of petrified limbs spilled in empty creek beds. Trees bled resin like rubies, sprouted goitrous nests, suspended cat's-cradles of spiderwebs, spinning disks of silk. Trees towered hard as bronze in still sunlight, and stirred like a living hide in the rolling advent of a storm.

If you were born to Runagate with all its fragile propriety, its tidy civilisation, its ring-fence of roads and paddocks, wires and blood, there was nothing else in the world beyond but trees.

CHAPTER ONE

LEMON TREE AND LANTERN-BUSH

My mother—pale, delicate Nerida Scott, who wilted like a garden in the heat of the day—did not like to speak of or even look at the trees beyond Runagate.

Our front garden—the prettiest-kept on Upper Spicer Street, the handsomest street in Runagate—contained nothing native to the ground from which we daily coaxed and tortured it. It was decent, tidy and ornamental, and, like my mother, gracious. Though she always sent me to borrow books for her on homemaking and manners and inspiring true stories, she didn't need them: Nerida Scott was as naturally elegant as a lily.

I, in contrast, had reached the age of nineteen, graceless and unlovely, despite our best efforts. There was too much of my father in me.

"But you are a good girl, aren't you?" said my mother, catching my hand with slender fingers when I stood to clear the lunch dishes. Her nails were smooth and petal-pink.

"Yes, Mother," I assured her. As I washed the plates, I concentrated on scrubbing out a little more, too, of that old childish self—the restless temper, the loose-limbed insolence I had got from my mocking father and unloving brothers, an unflattering pretension to cleverness. Unlearning the habits gained during the useless, featureless years I had spent at Runagate State School, before I had to grow up. Before I chose to. *Nothing* (she liked to say) is as unattractive as a woman with a *little* education, is it, Bettina? And I had spent three years resolutely becoming responsible and civilised and winsome. A strong will has its uses.

That day, like nearly every day, was bright. My mother, her eyes already green-shadowed with tiredness, settled to sleep. My mind quiet, I swept the kitchen to the companionable hum of the refrigerator, the midday crooning of red hens scratching beneath the lemons that hung in the backyard: lemons the size of ox hearts, thick-rinded, brilliant and knobby, luminous among the glossy green. They were not, I think, the shapely fruit my mother had expected, but she did not want to replace the tree. The scent wandered through the house. I would have gone and gathered armfuls of fragrant leaves, but my mother, in one of her few deviations from her magazines, considered cut arrangements gauche.

I washed my face and hands, carefully cleaned the dirt from beneath my nails, added the faintest of colours to my cheeks and lips, brushed the thick dull bob of my hair over the thread-thin scar, almost invisible, on my cheek—a childhood injury, forgotten—and straightened my skirt and blouse. My mother might be asleep, might not love her petty, parochial neighbours, but in Runagate she would certainly hear if I went out looking as if I had no one to care for me.

There had been no car at our house since the night my father left. My mother had barred my brothers from repairing their battered ute in the driveway, and in any event Mitch and Chris had soon gone too. But under the pressure of the midday sun, as I wheeled my yellow bicycle to the front gate, opened it and latched it neatly behind me, I almost regretted not being able to drive. Almost, but then a throbbing in my head and neck reminded me of what we had lost with it: the snarl and roar of engines in the garage and on the lawn, boys rioting through the house, light hair feathered white from the sun, shouting like crows, always too much in the open air. *Monsters!* my mother had called them, rightly: husband, sons, and cars too.

Nowadays our peace was broken only by wings outside the windows, the shifting of lace shadows. "We are pleasant together, aren't we, Bettina?" my mother would say, and I would answer, "Yes." We were homemakers; after everything, I chose to stay when restless spirits fled.

We bloom where we are planted. Don't we, Bettina? We are content. And I was content. For a moment, pushing back my hair at the door of the library before returning my mother's books (improving and inspiring), I smelled the ghost of oil and petrol sweet on my hands, but while I had few secrets from my mother, that was not a memory to grieve her with. It would fade.

I ran all my errands but one, and the bags swung heavy on the bicycle's handles.

"Scott-girl!" bellowed Pinnicke, the old scalper, on the corner before the petrol station, on the road leading away from Runagate. "I found something near the traps, dingo traps, I thought I'd got its paw—you'd think it would be a paw—but come see, come see."

I stepped down hard on the pedals, flew across the road and past the pumps, kicked the stand down quickly and darted into the shop.

"A hand!" laughed the old man, outside. "Complete with a ring!"

"Pinnicke bothering you, Bettina?" asked Casey Hale at the counter. She had cut off all her wild permed curls and her short hair was sleek. *Modern.*

"No, Miss Hale." Pinnicke was *quite unbalanced;* it was correct to avoid him, whatever acquaintance he'd scraped with my father. No one worth knowing had liked him. I scrambled to remember any of the old books on etiquette my mother had me read to her, but they didn't contemplate Pinnickes. I was breathing too fast. I'd hardly been acting my age.

"Bring your bike in," she said, too kindly. "You can leave through the back."

"No, thank you, Miss Hale." That would be undignified. "Is there a delivery for me, Miss Hale? From the bus?" *We don't end a sentence as if it is a question, do we, Bettina?* "From the bus," I corrected myself.

She raised one eyebrow—*vulgar,* my mother would have said, and once I would have wished I could do it—then went through a door and brought out a white box tied with baling twine and punched with holes. From inside, small voices cheeped.

"Are you sure?" she asked.

"Yes, Miss Hale. That is all, thank you."

I waited for her to give me the box. She gave me a long stare first. "Okay, *Miss Scott*." Her tone was rude, but at least she wasn't treating me like a child. "My compliments to your mum."

I accepted the box of chickens and bundled hastily outside again, narrowly avoiding a tall man with a sandy beard, and above it pale keen eyes, cold as a crow's. He smelled of blood and oil. *Not* from Runagate, I registered, and with speed (but not haste) stowed the box in the basket of my bicycle and fastened it there with cords.

"Reckon your dad would have been interested." Old Pinnicke was leaning against the wall. His breath stank like the air from the pub. "Always picking things up, wasn't he?"

The stranger had parked his ute—dented, rusted, piled with cages of geese and feathers—on what footpath there was. A two-way radio crackled inside the cab and something slumped low in the passenger seat, cowed, or dead. I pushed off the kerb into the road, where there were never cars.

Brakes screamed.

I stopped, hunched over the handlebars, eyes closed, waiting for my mind to catch up (surely it had once been *faster*). Curses from Old Pinnicke. A blue smell of rubber, like time contracting too fast. I opened one eye and saw a young man drop down from the cab of his red truck, rusty hair on end and freckles showing. This one was from Runagate. Too much so.

"Tina Scott!" said Gary Damson. "What the *hell* are you doing?"

But I was on the bicycle and away, my face hot as fire. I stood on the pedals, as if I were fifteen and heedless. I wanted

only to get out of the open street, the staring eyes of Runagate. To get to home and safety.

It was common knowledge (which is not the same as gossip)
that Mr Alleman, who lived next door, lost his son in the
Woodwild School fire before I was born. Since he'd retired
from covering clearing sales and dances for the *STAR*, he'd
found nothing better to do than watch his neighbours. His
sharp nose tracked above the leaves of his lantern-bush
hedge. "You've got a fan, Bettina Scott," he observed.

I intended to ignore him but could not avoid seeing what
he nodded to. Scrawled in black letters across our neat white
fence was the word *MONSTERS*.

"Who—" I began.

"I didn't see," said Mr Alleman, and tapped his blade of a
nose. "But we can guess, we can guess."

I couldn't. In spite of the heat, the paint stuck to my fingers. Fresh. Mr Alleman was chuckling. Chilled with fury,
I gathered the mail from our letterbox and went quickly
through the gate.

I settled the new chicks—no worse for the adventure with
the truck—under the hanging bulb, then lingered by the door
of the garage and sorted the mail, waiting for my mood to
settle, and Mr Alleman to lose interest and go indoors. A bill.
A flyer for events at the cultural centre: a bush-dance, an in-
troduction to computers, a water-dowsing workshop, a movie
to be shown on the last Saturday, and an historical lecture on
the eradication of invasive plants. *That* should be of interest to
Mr Alleman—we didn't approve of his garden. Letters to my
mother from her travelling friends in scripts looped, elegant

and feminine on flower-scented paper—I breathed it in, forcing myself to relax. The stamps read Åland, Ísland, Magyarország. Tiny bright worlds, smaller than Runagate, places where plants froze in the snow and died in the autumn. A catalogue of pretty throw-rugs and framed sayings, which we would look through after dinner. And a grubby little envelope, not stamped or post-marked, not even *addressed* except for one word: *TINK*.

You are truthful, Bettina, aren't you? I didn't answer, even to myself. That paper, that writing—filthy and bold and untidy—offended my already-ruffled spirit, and stirred it up like dirt at the bottom of a water tank. All my worst impulses.

This—whatever it was—was *mine*. I put it into the pocket of my skirt and stood in the garage, feeling my unsteady heart, and the paper resting guilty as fire against my leg. Mr Alleman had gone. My mother's advice would have guided me, but she was asleep, and for a moment the idea of rebelling against my own better judgement tasted as good as salt.

I scrubbed the fence, the sun hot through my blouse, the breeze pressing the fabric against my shoulder blades. But I could not enjoy that secret glory of movement and effort. My peace was twitched by my conscience, by the worry Mr Alle-man was watching behind his curtains, or my mother behind hers, by the growing suspicion this was not, in fact, the first letter I had received and therefore neither special nor deserv-ing of secrecy. Hadn't there been a letter once, ages ago, that my mother had read by the window, laughing softly to herself? The memory was sluggish, cobwebbed with disuse. It had been foolishness, my mother had said. *Nothing to bother our heads about, Bettina, is it?*

"Bettina Scott," said a voice behind me, angry and light, but a man's. I spun, spiralling dirty water. It spattered the driver's door of Gary Damson's truck, where the letters spelling Damson Fencing were peeling to reveal only their own deeper shadows. I was indecorously, bitterly, delighted. It was his own fault. He had startled me twice today.

"Was that *paint*?" he said. For a moment, my thoughts were fast enough: I was suddenly certain what Gary Damson's square hands would feel like, raised in anger. He leaped out, but I was taller and faster. Gathering bucket and brushes, I ran into the yard, past the house, back to the safety of the garage.

"You *coward*, Tina!" he shouted, voice cracking. I knew he would not follow. Mother had forbidden him the yard, back when my brothers left. Damsons respect fences.

Coward. My hands were shaking. "Hush," I whispered to myself, until they stilled, and my thoughts were quiet once more. I rinsed the bucket, and after a while the truck choked to life and roared away. Caution was better than bravery, I reminded myself. A civilised, bone-china soul knows, as a bird does, that a heavy-footed, shouting man is a thing to be fled.

The garage was quiet, except for the scrape and slide of noisy miner and magpie claws on the iron roof, the spreading patterns of hydrangea-blue shadows, and the perennial half-whispers in the trees that did not belong to any breeze or beast I had ever seen.

I wrung out the damp hem of my skirt, dried my hands and went inside.

"Are you feeling ill, Bettina?" my mother asked me in the bright evening, pausing over her letters.

"My stomach," I said. Unthinking, I rubbed my neck and shoulder.

"You mustn't be ill, Bettina," said my mother, anxious. "You are never ill." She smiled at me bracingly. "You are a good girl. You always do what I need to be done—you must be well for that. You are feeling better, aren't you?"

"Yes, Mother," I said. It had, after all, only been tension. Guilt, and alarm.

She paused delicately. "I heard some . . . altercation this afternoon."

"I'm sorry," I said. Her eyes were still shadowed. "Someone painted words on our fence. Not crude. Just 'monsters.' I cleaned it." Looking up, I saw her watching me, eyes kind and green, her pale lashes fine as the fringe on a fern.

"And?" she prompted.

"Gary—Mr Damson, young Mr Damson—came by."

"What did he want, Bettina?"

"I don't know," I said, honestly. "I didn't stay to ask."

My mother nodded. "The Damsons are no better than they should be," she said. "*Fencers.*" She shook her head, as if she did not love her white fence, as if the Damsons were involved in an arcane and dubious activity. "They are not like us, are they?"

"No, Mother."

She watched me.

"He shouted at me," I said, to please her, and to claw my way back to the peace I had felt that morning. *You always feel better when you tell the truth, don't you?* "For almost splashing paint on his truck. But he was the one who frightened me." Odd I had not heard him drive up. What had I been thinking of?

"Poor Bettina," said my mother. "Come here." She reached up and embraced me briefly; her skin was soft over the vine-firm tendons of her thin arms. A tightness I hadn't noticed in my back eased. There was, after all, nothing to worry about.

"Perhaps we should send that shock back where it belongs," said my mother.

She had ways—terribly polite, peaceful ways—of putting our world to rights. That night she called Sergeant Aberdeen, our policeman. I listened calmly, suppressing a juvenile glee. She thought he should know young Gary Damson was stirring up trouble; of course she could trust him to do what was necessary, couldn't she? He had a daughter, so he understood, after all?

We did not care for poor Winston's daughter, and so, "Did he understand?" I asked, when she hung up. My mother merely sighed. Patricia Aberdeen, after all, would have revenged herself upon Gary without recourse to the proper authorities.

"A shame he was saddled with raising such a wild girl," said my mother. "It was fortunate for everyone when she was sent away. Better not to think about her, don't you agree?"

So I did not. But when I changed for bed and emptied my pockets, I found the letter again.

It wasn't a real envelope. The paper was locked together by an untidy series of creases. With it a memory unfurled just as mechanically and rumpled: my hands knew this pattern, we had folded notes like this at school. *We? I* had been peculiarly friendless; it wasn't *nice* to have favourites, besides which the company at Runagate State School had been lacking. *Not like us.* Like Gary Damson, too much themselves: nothing but sunburn, muscle and dirt. Like my brothers.

A sudden image of the three of them, crow-hoarse with laughter, Mitch and Chris lanky as cranes beside Gary.

Dismissing that train of thought as unprofitable, I opened

the letter over my bare knees, the brittle butcher paper scraping faintly on faded scars.

It contained a page torn from the *Runagate, Woodwild and
Crossing STAR*. The date was three years old, but I guessed
each word before I read it.

YOUTHS RUN AMOK

DAMAGE AND DISTURBANCE

DESTRUCTION OF PEACE

I shifted the scrap to read the writing underneath: a large,
unsteady scrawl, the pen pressing veins into the paper.

YOU COWARD, TINK

Why would anyone trouble to point that out twice in one
day? Gary Damson's words, although he wouldn't have called
me *Tink*. Only my brothers and father had called me that.
But they were long gone. When I tried to remember how
their voices sounded when they said it, I couldn't. I wasn't surprised: even their faces were blurry. My mother hadn't kept
any photographs. *We don't need to be reminded, do we, Bettina?* Forgetting is easy, once you learn how.

I looked at the article again. It had been torn from its page,
with greasy thumbprints dark on the grey paper. It smelled
of motors and dung. I rested it back on my knees, holding it
cautiously so the newsprint could not come off too much on
my fingers.

Only my brothers.

I could have told my mother. But I lingered too long, and
felt through the house a draught, laden with the breath of growing things. Rain, I knew as if it had already fallen on me. A
serenity comes with that smell, calming the acid of doubt
and regret, stirring different thoughts. The scent of sharp
grass softening, the lemon tree digging its roots further
into the dissolving earth, the pepperina and lantern-bush

and beyond—pine, brigalow, eucalypt, the vast, uncivilising world shifting like a shaggy animal, silver-green under the clouds, dreaming, although my mother would not credit it, in memories.

TURNCOAT

This is a story I heard a long time later—or at least the bones of it.

Linda Aberdeen, formerly Spicer, had grown up in the city, married in the city, gone no further than the ocean for her honeymoon. The winter she headed west, she was first surprised at how far the city extended, then at how far beyond it the bus took her. Past the neat houses, the ragged houses, and the bulldozed plateaus with their spotless, pointless black streets. Beyond the dark green hills and the khaki hills. Out

to where the land unrolled vast and shimmering pale, or con-
tracted shaking and glittering into tunnels through which
their bus beat on.

Winston, with their baby Patricia fussing in his arms, saw
her off from the pebbled concrete transit centre early on a
damp morning, for even in winter, that city was never really
cold. "Why didn't you go with her?" was a question no one
would ask Winston Aberdeen as often as he would himself.

Late in the afternoon, the bus driver let Linda down onto
the beaded blue-and-red pebbles outside the mechanic's shop
at Carter's Crossing. Closed. There was a railway line but no
station, a few clean cream houses set clear of the grey trees, a
hall with CWA painted on it in looping blue, and the smallest
wooden church Linda had ever seen.

A man sat in the open back of a battered station wagon,
smoking. He was wearing scuffed sneakers instead of boots—
not at all what Linda had expected.

"Darryl Scott?" she asked, checking the letter from her
grandmother.

He drove her another hour—it felt longer. The bitumen
ended; the wheels struck white dirt with a drumming like a
racing heart.

"Sylvie doesn't clear that track anymore" was all Darryl
Scott bothered to say, when he dropped her beside the road.
"You can walk from here."

He tossed her duffle bag down beside her and was off again,
leaving her coughing in dust fine as powder. He admitted it
later, when pressed. No reason to deny it. They hadn't talked
much. She wasn't his type. He had not seen a woman answering Linda Aberdeen's description again.

"It's only a visit," said Linda to herself, choking on dry
air. "Anyone can visit their grandmother." Still she wished

she had brought her daughter with her, if only as something warm to hold.

Here, the air was dry as paper and chilly. There were no houses to redirect the wind that flew along the road and through her green coat, tangled her hair and stung her nose. No buildings visible at all. No cars. Nothing Linda knew.

Sylvie Spicer had sent Linda a firmly drawn map with *Keep on the path* written in bold black letters. The only other landmarks on it were the road, "Blue Mailbox Corner", "The Dead Tree" and "Creek." It took Linda several minutes to find the mailbox, although it was no longer blue: a tin-roofed wooden box, large enough to hold a child, cobwebbed and filled with purple shadow. The path began there: a crease in the brittle grass barely wider than Linda's shoe. No gate.

She clambered through the slack wires of the boundary fence—the fluted wood of the posts shifting slightly with the disturbance—slung her bag over her shoulder and set off down the slope toward the trees that seemed to indicate a watercourse.

Throughout the long bus ride and the days leading to it, Linda had fought to lower her expectations. Her beautiful, tormented, uneasy mother, both kleptomaniacal when it came to superstitions and deeply suspicious of all fiction, had never spoken of Sylvie Spicer. It was too easy for Linda to hope Sylvie might be everything her own mother had not been, everything she wanted to learn to be for Patricia.

But the interminable drive, the cracked cold land, the wire-sharp grass abraded those hopes.

"Still," Linda said to herself and a flitting wagtail, "blood and water, and all that." At least, Winston had said, it would let her stop wondering about her mother's family.

The grass she strode through clung to her jeans and

hemmed her coat in pale seeds. She strained to see an opening, a gate, another fence in the trees, anything that hinted at a destination, but the air stung her eyes to tears. When she lowered her hand, she saw the animal.

Linda had never seen a dog that colour, the peculiar grey-blonde of the grass, like ash and honey. Its limbs were thin, its skull narrow and its eyes glass-green: brilliant and alive. Metres away from the track, it watched her, every part motionless: its small ears, the hollow-flanked body tapering to a skeletal tail. The only thing she knew for certain, bone-deep, blood-deep, was *It can run faster than me.*

She stood, staring. A tremor ran through it, something more than the ruffle of its coat in the wintery air.

All the stories her mother had not cared to tell her, the stories Linda had begun to read to her own daughter, bristled along her spine. Wild woods—oak or deodar or cedar, depending on which of her mother's histories she chose to plumb, for she wasn't on a sure footing with Winston's family's stories yet—where nightmares stalked their prey; stories to keep children from wandering, to brighten the lights of home. Abruptly, they made unwelcome, visceral sense. Linda scrabbled desperately through them for advice. *Don't visit your grandmother* was unhelpful, and too late.

She thought through the contents of her pockets: bus ticket, chewing gum, comb. The pocket knife Winston gave her before they were married, engraved *LS* and too stiff for her to open quickly, even if she could have done much damage with it, was in her bag. And the letter, with *Keep on the path* written so heavily she could feel it from both sides of the paper.

Keep on the path, even if golden-silver death watched you with green glass eyes, beautiful fur showing every line of its ribs.

"Good boy," said Linda, and stepped forward.

The fur shifted on its back like grass in the wind.

There was nowhere to run. No vehicle had passed them on the white dirt road from Carter's Crossing; to each side of the world trees piled paper-dry onto the horizons. But ahead ought to be Sylvie Spicer's house. Besides, in those nearer trees Linda might find a handy branch.

She fitted her foot carefully into the track. A long, low vibration started in the creature's throat.

Linda gripped the handle of her bag, ready to swing it, and stepped again. The animal jerked forward, quicker than Linda wanted ever to remember. A metre away, it stopped, head down.

"Damn, you're fast," said Linda. She rubbed one sweating palm against her coat. "But you're not coming any closer. Are you trained? Not to let trespassers in? Sit!" she said, experimentally. Nothing happened.

"If you're Sylvie Spicer's idea of a guard-dog," said Linda, lifting her chin, "she has a few things to learn about hospitality." She brandished the letter. "I'm family. I'm invited, I'll have you know!"

At her next step, she heard grass cracking under her foot and wrenched her gaze away just in time to catch herself, step down on dirt instead. When she looked up, the creature was on the other side of the path. She hadn't heard it jump.

"Watch me," said Linda, forgetting she was an adult, and a mother. "I grew up walking park railings."

The animal flitted over the ground like a shadow, always at the corner of her eye, keeping a steady distance. Linda didn't put a foot wrong.

After a long, whispering silence, the low vibration began

again, a note that climbed steadily into a high keening. As the sound rose, the wind swept down from the hills. A cold, arid gale stripped tears from Linda's eyes and whipped her hair across her face. It tore at her coat and snatched her letter away, spinning it tumbling and catching across the paddock.

She stopped herself on the point of leaping after it and looked back to see the animal at her heels, unblinking. "Two not out," said Linda against the icy wind. "All I have to do is stay on the path."

She made it to the trees. Later, they would find a thread of her coat caught on the bark of a dead silky oak, although they would not know whether she had left it coming or going. The animal, breathing at her heels, began a tuneless moaning, varying notes and sobbing howls, coarser than birdsong, more deliberate than the rush of water.

She tried to ignore it, not to find a pattern, but there were— feelings. Impressions of violet shadows and chill golden sunlight, the twisting nets of liquid day through brown water, the scudding lights of high clouds at dawn, the blazing of stars in blue nights and beneath all that, echoes of darkness like centuries in rocks, and the promise of the unknown behind bleak hills.

The late afternoon sky, the sharp air and the track shifted, dissolved together. Linda put her hands over her ears. "I can't hear you!" she lied loudly, and hurried through the susurration of she-oaks. The animal bounded lightly beside her, the brindles of its coat flickering. Linda stumbled through the trees until the ground gave way.

She lay at the bottom of a dry creek bed, bruised and dusty. At the top of the bank from which she had fallen was a fence: a tottering row of pickets knotted together by clawed bushes, broken where she had fallen through. The animal looked down at her, the whitening hairs around its muzzle clear, twitched one ear, then sauntered—almost hopped—out of sight.

Linda dusted herself off, limped up the other side and between the trees. There was no beast waiting. Only brown and black chooks hunting insects in the grass, a vegetable garden and a tired grey house, bowed with age.

She had expected a woman as dark as her own mother. But the old lady who pulled the door in, scraping it over the curl of mustard-yellow linoleum, was tall and green-eyed.

"Sylvie Spicer?" hazarded Linda.

"Good lord," said the older woman—too old, surely—opening the screen door. "You're the image of your mother."

"She wasn't my daughter," said Sylvie Spicer.

In the kitchen with its bleached mock-marble Formica and floral linoleum, with a gun above the door and an electric stove set into the recess where a wood stove must have once stood, Sylvie Spicer had cleaned up the scrapes on Linda's hands, anointing them with yellow iodine. Now she served tinned fruitcake in the living room. The sinking furniture was crowded by low shelves of curling farm annuals, condensed novels, an aged encyclopaedia and a few curious titles such as *In the Wake of Sea Serpents* and *The Fables of Mkhitar Gosh*.

"That was my son. We lost him." The boy in the picture with its curved glass frame was holding a rifle and not exactly a boy. He wasn't in uniform, but Linda, not used to seeing rifles in snapshots, assumed a war took him. Korea, perhaps? The frame was older than the picture. He looked like a clever young man; he might have been an amusing uncle. But he wasn't Linda's uncle, and Sylvie had never been her grand-mother. A dusty, stale grief sat in the hollow of Linda's throat.

Sylvie went on. "They found his clothes and gun, but no sign of him. Then your mother arrived. Washed up in the creek after the rain. I almost hated her for taking poor David's place. Strange girl. Never liked to say where she'd been before us, and didn't stay long after. But she was the only thing I had left to love."

"She loved me," said Linda, as she had told herself many times. She needed to believe it—she had lost any claim she hoped to have on Mrs Spicer, and the ache surprised her. Still, the old woman had invited her here. Maybe she was lonely. A foster-grandmother was better than none. "Do you have any photos of her?"

"No," said Mrs Spicer.

Linda pulled out her wallet. "I have one in here—not very good, she never did like cameras—you can have it. If you want."

"My memory will serve. What happened on the path?"

In the ordinariness of the house, it all seemed half-imagined. "Your dog," said Linda. "I'm frightened of dogs. They always seemed to be barking at us when I was little. I was startled, and fell into the creek."

"I don't keep a dog," said Mrs Spicer flatly, and stood to carry the teapot back to the kitchen.

Linda glanced around for a telephone. Perhaps Darryl Scott, taciturn as he was, could take her back to Carter's Crossing. There must be somewhere to wait for a bus back to the coast.

"Silver-brown?" Mrs Spicer asked from the kitchen.

"Yes," said Linda. "With pale eyes. Like bottle-glass."

"It must have liked you," said Sylvie Spicer, bitter as the tea. "It doesn't usually show itself so readily. Called, did it?"

Linda, listening to evening gathering outside, remembered how the sound had seemed anchored to the roots of the world. "Is it dangerous?"

"Of course it is," said Sylvie Spicer sharply, reappearing in the doorway. "Dangerous itself, and dangerous because of those looking for things like it." She looked Linda up and down, in a familiar way, and sniffed. "He must have known you were hers."

"Mum left here before I was born," said Linda. "Dogs don't live that long. Do they?"

"You know it wasn't a dog," said Mrs Spicer. "My family's been settled here a long time, Linda Aberdeen." Her green eyes flashed, as if she expected Linda to challenge that claim. "We aren't given to wandering. Something like this has been around a long time too. People vanish. It changes. This pale one has been here since your mother arrived. Since David disappeared."

"I thought he went to war."

"War?" said Sylvie, contemptuous. "He went up to the top paddock—him and his dogs—and only his horse came home. Never a bit of use afterwards." She looked severely at Linda. "Blood calls to blood."

Linda studied the photo in her wallet, slid it back into her bag. "You're saying that . . . creature *ate* David?"

"In a manner of speaking," said Mrs Spicer, with a thin smile.

"I've called that nice Mr Scott," said Mrs Spicer. "He'll drop you in Woodwild. The Stockman's Arms is still open, last I heard. If they'll take you."

"Thank you," said Linda, measured. The woman was

unbalanced—by loneliness and grief, perhaps—and Linda wasn't going to antagonise her unnecessarily. But she wasn't going to stay. "I'll wait by the road."

"You don't want to walk it in the dark," conceded Mrs Spicer. Linda could have done without that thought.

She shouldered her bag and strode away, furious and—yes, miserable. Stupid! She *had* a family. Winston and Patricia, the extended, extensive network of Aberdeen brothers and sisters, aunts and uncles. And yet . . . the creature had known her. What if—only for the sake of a story, mind—what if it had understood when she said she was family? Out there all alone for years and years, never able to come in, watching its people grow old and die?

The last light threaded thin and gold through the trees by the creek, flinging long blue shadows over the tossing grass. It smelled of distant smoke, of new-broken leaves and— although the creek was dry—dark water. Starveling country, her mother had called this. Whatever the truth of it, her mother had *wanted* to be from somewhere else.

Linda stood in the paddock, between the creek and the fringe of trees that hid the road. The sky was mother-of-pearl.

"Hello?" she said to the fading light, feeling foolish. She cleared her throat. "I only want to talk."

The path, in this light, was the scratch of a nail. A brief, battening gust of wind stung her face. She dropped her duffle bag, pulled off her coat and pushed up her sleeve with hands still yellow with iodine. Mrs Spicer hadn't bandaged the scrapes—it only cost Linda a little pain to bring red blood beading. The cold soon numbed it. *What are you doing, Linda Aberdeen?* The scent of her blood, and her mother's.

"I'm here," she whispered, hoping nothing would answer. "I've come." She turned and saw the beast.

Its pale eyes were bright as lamps with the last sun, its head low; the shadows along its ribs moved and flickered as it breathed.

It did not simply stand on the earth, thought Linda. It was part of the light and the wind, the scrubby trees, the bony hills. It contained them. She could smell the creature: earth and plants, blood and wildness. It lowered its narrow jaw and let out a high, rippling keening.

"Oh, you poor beautiful thing," said Linda, and stepped off the path.

The creature sprang, but Linda expected that. She caught it bodily—much bigger than a child, but she had learned to hold tight. It was not ethereal now: its fur was greased and matted, its hot carnivorous breath snapped too near her throat. She could not let go. She could never let go. She'd have laughed, if she'd had breath.

Here I am waiting, Mr Scott, and a little something I picked up. I'm sorry, Winston, it followed me home.

Its claws tore her sleeve, and it changed beneath her touch, convulsing and contorting, bones and joints shifting into a creature stranger and ill-formed, multi-limbed, scaled and furred, bat-leathered, draggle-feathered. There *had* been something in the fruitcake, thought Linda distantly.

When it stopped struggling, the stars had moved on and the moon had risen. The face looking down at hers was a young man's, though grooved with weariness and hunger. He was wrapped in her coat. All Linda's strength had leached into the chilly earth.

"What did the old witch tell you, to make you do that?" he said, wondering. The moon silvered his hair—or was it whitening? It haloed him too brightly for mere moonlight, and the shadows around were peculiarly deep and clear, warm-hued beneath him as much as beneath the grasses, as if the same blood flowed through both. The lines on his face had deepened. He wasn't as young as she'd thought.

"Nothing," Linda tried to say, but her voice betrayed her: a broken wheeze that wrapped around her heart and clenched, cold. When she reached for him, her arm felt numb and gloved.

She struggled from the grass and, resting a moment—for the last moment she still thought her life had not changed unutterably—saw a flutter of contempt in his face. He turned, clutching the coat around him, and ran, limping, his legs sinewy white beneath its hem.

Linda leapt up, tangled in the torn remnants of her shirt, and struggled backwards out of it, out of all her clothes, plunging bodily into the night wind that fluttered the hair on her arms and back and ribs. Through the soles of her feet and hands, through her skin, the land sang to her: dark and silver, the bones of the world. She felt the drumming of David Spicer's bare feet, outdistancing her easily. At the edge of the creek, he stopped. She could not feel what lay beyond those pickets: the house was outside her visible world and Sylvie Spicer, waiting, was only a wavering shade.

"Do you think I don't remember you?" said David, to Linda, or to what Linda had become. His voice was harsh. *He's old,* she thought, and then, *He thinks I'm my mother.* "You tricked me, but you've had your go. You've taken my life and all these years. Do you know what it's like to watch the world turning and passing and never taking you with it? You've had your time walking it. Take your own back."

David stepped down into the crossing, and from the opposite bank a spasm threaded the air, furrowing cold and then heat along her ribs. *A bullet,* realised Linda, as the sound cracked in her ears. *Just like the movies.*

She turned and ran, on four unruly legs. Lights on the road. She raced to it, scrabbled belly to the grass beneath the wires, dashed out. The station wagon was high, huge. She could see the long road beneath and beyond it, pale with stars.

"Mr Scott!" she tried to call, once. A billowing of fumes and throbbing on the air, and the car moved to where she stood caught in the beams. It struck her side. Had she not spent her life in traffic, had Darryl Scott accelerated faster, she might have been killed. As she reeled into the trees on the other side of the road, panic began to wash her away. The old earth, the inevitability of blood and fear, the quicksilver heartbeat of the lonely stones rose into her. She ran blindly into the hills.

CHAPTER TWO

THESE ARE GOLD

In the morning, in the clear stillness of the world after rain, I pulled a short-sleeved cardigan over my sundress, wrapped a shred of courage around the great betrayal of the letter, and went out. I had no proof of anything to go upon. Only the dislodged memories of *monsters* and notes passed in school (by whom I could not imagine), and that newspaper dated the week my father left us, and a very few people I could ask about the word painted on our fence.

"Why would I tell you?" said Mr Alleman, over the lantern-bush hedge, spikes between the hollow flowers. He gave his thin, yellow smile. "What would you give me to tell you?"

I knew no answer with which to dignify that.

The postmaster, who lived on Lower Spicer Street, was pulling weeds from the rain-soft earth in the shadow of his water tank.

"Hello, Bettina," he said gravely, as he had since I was small. "And how are you this morning? Keeping up with your practice?"

I stared at him.

"Piano," he supplied at last.

A memory of sweat behind my knees, my toes just brushing brass pedals and Mrs Sage precise beside me saying, "Raise your hands like you're holding apples, Tina! If you drop your wrists, the wolves will get them." I looked in surprise at my knuckles, white where I held on to the handlebars. My mother didn't even like me to hum.

"Never mind," he sighed. "Was there something Nerida wanted?"

"N-no," I said. "It's me. I. I wondered—only, perhaps it was a prank. I don't like to worry my mother." Perhaps I had only imagined that I was bold once.

"No one likes that," said Mr Sage.

"Was there an envelope for me?" I hurried on, before caution or shyness could overwhelm me. "A little dirty folded one? It was in the mailbox."

"No," said Mr Sage. "I'd remember a letter to you, Bettina."

I bit my lip. There was only one other person to ask.

"Try Gary Damson," advised Mr Sage. I flinched, guiltily. "He won't bite, Tina. Those notes from Gary are the only mail I ever remember for you. And if not him—well, sometimes he brings things into town for people. I'd take him to task for cutting in on my business, except he takes the mail run over in bad weather. Steadier than I expected him to turn out, all in all. Ask him."

My mother always said, *You are truthful, aren't you, Bettina?* I'd always answered, *Yes, Mother.* With an effort, I said, "If I see him. Thank you, Mr Sage."

I looked over my shoulder as I turned the corner. He was shaking his head over his nasturtiums.

I'd avoided Gary Damson for so long that I knew exactly how to get to his house. It stood outside of town, past the showgrounds; within the paddocks circling Runagate, but too near the trees. Not a short ride.

My legs were shaking by the time I stopped at the bottle tree by the Damsons' gate. The gate was open, but a cattle grid cut the road and I found I did not want to ride over it.

I stood and worried. There were things I should be doing at home. I had left early, but my mother would notice if I stayed away long or came home flushed and sweating. She was unpredictable after rain, by turns effusive and sleepy. I could just go home, where all was pleasant and orderly. Not at all like the scrubby yard at the end of the Damsons' long dirt driveway, cluttered with sheds and machines, swings and toys.

Gary's truck pulled out from behind the house and my fledgling curiosity failed. I fled, but Gary covered the drive and the short stretch of road I'd put behind me and caught up easily, idling along behind until I pulled over, furious with embarrassment. I slithered down the shoulder to stop, one ankle deep in the muddy ditch.

"Hello, Tina," said Gary. The window was down, his elbow high on the door. He didn't smile.

I scrambled haughtily up from the mud. Mother would know now that all my efforts to change myself hadn't worked, unless I could wash my tyres and shoe at the showgrounds. But the woken questions lingered. I drew the shabby envelope from my pocket. "Did you deliver this, Mr Damson? Mr Sage said you had sent letters to us before."

He reached for it, but I didn't give it to him, and he didn't answer my question.

"Did you ride all the way here?"

"Yes."

"Does your mum know?"

I looked at my muddy shoe.

Gary sighed. "Put the bike in the back," he said. "I'll drop you home. I'll tell you what I know."

At least being a homemaker meant I was strong. As I wrestled the bicycle onto the truck's tray between the tin trunks bolted to the bed, the jerry cans tied to the sides, I saw Gary watching me in the mirrors. He didn't offer to help, or open my door.

The seats were worn, the floor thick with dirt and grease. I touched as little as possible as I climbed in, but the door was stiff and didn't close properly. Gary reached across to loosen and slam it. I flattened myself away from his arm.

The seatbelt wouldn't buckle. "Hold on," he suggested.

"You aren't a gentleman," I said, sitting straight-backed, the better to look down on him.

"So I've been told." He glanced back over his shoulder, toward his house, then started forward. I *wanted*, wildly and irrationally, the seatbelt.

"The note?" I prompted.

"What about it?"

"You said you'd tell me."

"I said I'd tell you what I know. Which is nothing."

I clenched my hands, feeling fifteen—no, *twelve* again. "You tricked me!"

"Used to be harder. When did it arrive?"

My nails had dug crescents in my palm. I smoothed them over my skirt. "Yesterday."

"Trish arrived yesterday. Not her writing?"

"How would I know?" I asked, genuinely surprised.

"What about the writing on your fence? The same?"

"Most people write rather differently with brushes than they do with pens, Mr Damson," I said primly.

"Could be anyone," he mused as we passed the show-grounds. Too fast. I wasn't used to being in a truck, or to speed: perhaps I had succeeded in growing up, after all. "Nobody much likes you Scotts."

"We're hardly *Spicers*."

He shrugged. "Nearly everyone's married into the Spicers at some point. I wouldn't put too much store by that. Otherwise—what about old mate at the truck stop yesterday? The crazy one, with the dog in the passenger seat? If it was a dog. Something hairy."

It might have been a man, slumped low.

I shivered. "How would he know—"

"Know what?"

"To call me Tink," I said. Gary didn't answer. It was a foolish hope. "And why would a stranger hate us?"

"Ask your mother," said Gary. "Any point in asking who *she* thinks did it?"

I opened my mouth, closed it again. Of course I should. She would take the whole question away, tell me not to fret. But the question was *mine*. "I didn't want to trouble her," I said. "Mr Sage said—"

"About that," said Gary, and pulled over to the side of the road. He turned to face me. Anyone could see us. They'd tell my mother and she would know that, hard as I tried, there was still rot at the core.

"Please keep driving," I said.

"Trish said you never wrote."

"To *her*?"

"What did she do? What did *I* do? And don't say *you know*, because I don't. Look, Tina, it's been three years. I've got to get back before *my* mum gets mad, let alone yours. She's not pleased with Mrs Scott, let me tell you. Calling the *police*."

"I really ought to be getting home," I said, with awful politeness.

"You can walk, or you can answer my question: *What happened the night your dad disappeared?*"

I was bewildered. Nothing had happened. He had just— gone. I ought to be afraid of Gary Damson, I thought faintly. I'd run from him yesterday, and he was angry now. But I was remembering how Gary brought the newspaper to show us that headline, laughing and heartless, and made my mother white-angry. My face warmed: her fury at my brothers was such a private thing to have overheard. A Family Matter. The sort of thing polite people, if they chanced to overhear, never mentioned.

"I'll ride home," I said.

But Gary hit the accelerator. The tyres sprayed gravel, and I closed my eyes, hands braced on the glovebox.

The taste of blood, the smell of burned rubber.

"Stop, I'll tell you! She-was-angry-with-them-and-with-my-father-for-encouraging-them-and-they-fought-and-he-left." Words sharp as shattered glass. That was it; I had that right.

The truck no longer felt so dangerously fast. I opened one eye, then the other. A vision of wheeling stars vanished. We were proceeding almost sedately through town. I smoothed my hair, sat up straighter.

"What about you?" he said. His blunt fingers drummed on the wheel.

"Me?"

"Was she angry with you?"

You were home asleep, like a good girl, weren't you, Bettina?

"Why would she be?" I said coldly.

We stopped in front of my house. Gary looked at me in disgust.

"Thank you for the lift, Mr Damson," I said with as much dignity as I could manage, and climbed out. I hauled the bicycle from the back and dropped it onto the road with a damaging bounce.

"You *are* a coward," he said. "We covered for you, you know."

I wheeled the bicycle to the garage, hosed off the crusting mud, checked the new chicks cheeping contentedly under their lamp, and went to sit by the lemon tree until I was calmer and my shoe was dry. Bees were heavy around my shoulders and hair. They rose on the warm morning air up to the windows, the gutters.

My mother would hear Gary Damson had been by our house. Twice in two days, causing trouble where none was wanted. But this time, I—mature, sensible Bettina—had gone looking for him. To spare her. To spare myself. *You coward, Tink.*

The kitchen smelled of lemon curd and toast, as I had left it. My note—*Out For Milk*—lay untruthful on the table. Blight on a perfect leaf. The stairs settled heavily as I went up.

The scent of citrus and too-sweet smoke thickened as I eased open the door of my mother's room. She was fully dressed, shoes and stockings on, her feet neatly together. A faint smile bloomed on her lovely face, yet I hated seeing her asleep, hollow as a cicada shell, as a lantern-flower. Her letters lay open on the bed. She could hardly leave Runagate and me, but it felt as if she were a world away. If only for a few hours, she too had left me.

The empty house dragged me down like wet clothes. Once, it had shaken daily with voices and running feet. *Dreadfully untidy.* I looked at the old scars on my hands, my knees. Almost vanished, scattered faint as fireworks, as gravel . . .

You coward . . . Gary *must* know something. I was calmer. Perhaps if I asked him again, nicely.

At the telephone table, I paged through the slim directory, seeking the Damsons. What were Gary's parents' names? They caught at the edge of memory, then came free: Brian and Marilyn. Between *V Damson* (only an address in Woodwild, no phone) and *KL Danville* (the auctioneer), a heavy black line had been ruled neatly through the name, address and number of *B & M Damson*. I flipped the book around, but the advertisement for Damson Fencing wasn't there, either.

I couldn't call the directory—my mother might hear me ask for the Damsons' number—and I could hardly borrow a phone book from Mr Alleman.

I chewed my thumbnail, then opened the drawer and took out my mother's address book. The Damsons weren't there, of course, but I was sure Sergeant Aberdeen, who had the only unlisted number, had been. There were no names at all under *A*, but no sign of anything having been erased. I flipped back through and found him under *W*, for *Winston*, smoothed the book open, stared at the phone's dial, took a deep breath and lifted the handset.

I did not breathe while the phone rang. My heart thundered. *Don't answer,* I willed down the line. *Don't.* It rang and rang. I was about to hang up, relieved, when I heard a click.

"Yep?" said a young woman. She sounded as if she were chewing gum. *Unsanitary and unattractive.*

"Hello?" I said, deciding, with difficulty, against introducing myself until I knew to whom I was speaking. It felt excitingly clandestine. "May I please speak with Patricia Aberdeen?"

"This is Trish," she answered.

I clutched the receiver with both hands and said, "Hello, Patricia. This is Bettina Scott speaking."

I thought the line had dropped. Then Patricia Aberdeen swore.

AND WHAT
LIVES IN THEM

"There aren't any stories except the ones we bring with us," Trish Aberdeen used to say, stamping into the long grass after school, as if she wanted it to be true (as if she didn't keep thinking she'd seen wolves and tigers stalking her in the scrub). Gary Damson, who knew better, who suspected Trish knew better too, would hold his tongue.

Because even if she were right, *something* had to happen to all the stories no one wanted. Histories and memories that had been taken into the trees, beyond the fences and roads—those seams of the world from which reason and civilisation leak—and abandoned.

They must have outnumbered all the living population of

Inglewell. Stories that had belonged to the people who lived there before the Spicers established Runagate Station (*not*, as Trish Aberdeen took pains to point out, *her* people, because her dad wasn't from this part of the country at *all*, and who knew where her mother was from, maybe Spain or India, maybe she was a *princess,* and she had hit my brother Chris for laughing at her—she was always hitting Chris). Battles, massacres, murder; bushrangers and lonely revenge; tales of whose last stand was on this knob of land, of what will catch the toes of children swimming unattended, of witches in the scrub waiting for the unwary, of loping beasts and whispering megarrities. Then there were stories of those who had simply . . . gone. Walked into the trees or vanished from a tent in the night, been swallowed up in long-fingered leaves, waded into waterholes or fallen through cracks in the earth. Or those who had got into the car one night and driven off without saying goodbye. *What do we care, Bettina? It only proved what we knew of them. Heartless.*

Those histories, those memories, looped around Inglewell, a fence as rusted and relentless as any other. How could you think of leaving your lost and dead? And if you left, could you ever truly be gone?

CHAPTER THREE

SHINING THROUGH THE TREES

This wasn't defiance, I told myself half an hour after calling the Aberdeens. I was nineteen, after all. It was hardly *unbecoming* to care a little about what happened to my own brothers. The cooking brandy in the cupboard had tasted like nothing so much as dead air, and hardly strengthened my resolve. I slipped from the yard, trailing guilt, and rounded the corner. There, a third appearance of Gary Damson would be less likely to be noticed by my mother or the neighbours.

I had asked Trish Aberdeen to pass a message to Gary, and I expected him to arrive alone, but Trish was in the passenger seat of the truck, hanging on to the handle above the door. The sinews and tendons of her naked arm stood out. She was wearing a singlet and—I saw when she pushed the door open and slid closer to Gary—very short shorts, and boots.

"Hello, Patricia," I said.

Birds laughed in the gardens along the street. After a long moment, Trish said, "Get in, Tina."

"I don't think I will, thank you."

"Well, it's not the fanciest transport," said Trish, "but— Is that a *picnic basket*?"

Trish *would* be unprepared, I thought. Dressed like that. Her black hair curled wildly and a wolf was tattooed on her brown shoulder. *Déclassé*.

I held the container of sandwiches hard against my stomach and wished I had not started this train of events.

"*Technically*," said Gary, "it's Tupperware." I realised he was trying not to laugh. Trish drove an elbow at him.

"Do you want our help or not?" said Trish. "I don't know about your mum, but Gary's is Not Impressed. Get in."

They can't make me! The violence of the thought startled me. *Gently, Bettina. They cannot make you lose your temper.* I could still change my mind.

I stepped forward. The late-morning sunlight rose from the road, thick as molasses. Easier to stay home, where I knew what would happen, what would be said. But that spark of temper hadn't died, and I was angry at my own reluctance. Trish raised her eyebrows. She was wearing mascara. I could see where it crusted on her eyelashes. I could smell her deodorant. A lady tried never to smell of anything except a hint of flowers.

I wrenched myself forward, scrambled in and slammed the door behind me. My heart was beating hard, but I sat stiffly, hands clasped on top of the container, trying not to press against Trish's bare shoulder.

Trish stared at my dress. "Hold on" was all she said. The truck bolted forward and I caught at the handle as we tore down the street, all crowded together far too close for comfort. Too close for me to slide down out of sight of the neighbours, even if it was unladylike. Last time, we must have been smaller. *Last time?* I shouldn't have come, I realised. Clearly I wasn't well. I should stay home.

Too late. We were nearly through town, then onto the highway. Surely we were far above the speed limit. My stomach was falling away.

Gary drove with his elbow on the edge of the open window, fingers tapping a pattern on the side of the door. Trish slid down in the seat and put her boots on the dashboard, wrists resting loosely on her knees. From time to time she glanced at me, at the scar on my cheek. I looked out the window. I didn't remember ever truly leaving Runagate. The tidy houses, the high blue-white water tower, the historic windmill, the shouldering silos folded quickly and vanished behind tossing trees.

"I asked around," said Gary. "The only strangers in town yesterday were two men picking up geese at Hale Motors. I didn't get a good look at them. Did you?"

I shook my head. People can change a lot, even in three years, and I barely remembered my brothers' faces.

"*Geese?*" said Trish.

"Bus delivery," explained Gary.

"The bush is weird," said Trish, as if she hadn't lived half her life here. She grimaced at the clouds of gold and green leaves billowing at the top of a cutting.

"Casey Hale said one of them slunk off and the other was

jumpy about it, so they could have been the ones who wrote on Tina's fence."

"Opportunity," said Trish, "but hardly motive." She glanced at me critically. Part of me was still standing on the roadside in Runagate, listening to their voices far away. I wanted to retreat: into myself, into my mother's arms.

"She said they drove in from Carter's Crossing to pick up the delivery, since the bus doesn't go there," said Gary. "Margie at the Crossing doesn't have the phone on, but it's not too far"—Trish looked pointedly at my sandwiches—"we can find out who they are, clear all this up."

"Which is no more than any intelligent person could have discovered," said Trish. "Why didn't you let her make her own investigations?"

I didn't catch Gary's reply. His voice was faint as bees.

Saplings and taller trees and overarching boughs, the swoop and dip of wires, like the lope of something keeping pace with us. Cages of alternating shadow and brilliance. The sun hot through the window, like a greenhouse, like a glass coffin. My nose and lips felt numb. My heart clenched.

"Oh, stop— Gary, pull over!" Trish's voice was muffled. I was retching out of the door and then I was down from the truck, wrist-deep in thick, soft dust, pebbles against my knees, grass pricking my shoulders through my cardigan's short sleeves. I dug my fingers into the earth.

"We drive for five minutes . . ." grumbled Gary.

"Let it out," said Trish. Her rough fingers, gathering back my hair, were unpleasantly familiar. I shrugged her away. I was empty. I wanted my mother there to say all was well, don't worry. But she was asleep in Runagate. Only the sun rested like a hand on my head and the back of my dress and my legs. I breathed in the sleeping-animal smell of the grass, the dirt pressed with the questing arrows of birds, the slim prints of wallabies, the sweep of scales, the rounded fist of paws scratched by the tips of nails. Most so small or narrow, but here one large as the palm of my own hand, there the crescent of a hoof. The drumming of earth.

No—Gary starting the engine. I staggered to my feet. Trish passed me a green plastic water canteen and looked at me narrowly.

"I'm well," I lied. But I was better. Trish grunted. Back inside, she made me keep the window open, although the wind tangled my hair.

"It's quiet in here," said Trish over the roar of air. She poked at the radio. No sound emerged. "Something's stuck in the cassette player. Why aren't you talking, Gary?"

"I'm pissed off at you," said Gary, without conviction. "Why aren't *you* talking?"

"Because *Betty* here thinks I'm bad company."

"Tina," Gary corrected her.

"Bettina," I said, and added, "I never said that." Not in so many words.

"Then you aren't observant," said Trish. "I bet you cross the street rather than walk past the pub." She hoisted herself up in the seat and pulled cigarettes and a lighter from the pocket, such as there was, of her shorts.

"Not in here, Trish," said Gary.

"Betty wouldn't mind, would you, Betty?" she said. "Or—no, wait, let me guess, you don't smoke, either." She flicked the lighter a few times. "All right. That's the reunion. *So* glad I came home for the holidays."

"Why *are* you here, Trish?" I asked coolly.

She stretched her legs. "The primary appeal of Runagate

is nothing happens. Two television stations. I don't think they've heard of the internet."

"There's a new terminal at the cultural centre," volunteered Gary.

Trish ignored him. "Then suddenly Tina Scott, responsible for all the trouble I ever got in from my dad, and who hasn't spoken to me in—well, a long time—calls. So what, I ask, is the emergency?"

"Nothing," I said at the same time as Gary said, "Her brothers."

"Chris?" said Trish, with an odd tone. "And Mitch? Are they back in town?"

"Maybe. Or someone who knows them well enough to bother stirring things up."

"It's probably nothing," I said firmly. Such a foolish hope to start a journey on.

"Better not be nothing," said Gary. "I'll bill you for the fuel."

I still felt numb, but my head was clearer. Gary had made enquiries. He wouldn't be driving all this way if he hadn't thought there was a chance Mitch and Chris had come home—I resolutely did not think of my father. Gary and Trish wouldn't come along because they liked *me*.

"That's why you're still in town?" she asked. "I thought you'd bolt as soon as they opened the gate. You're bright enough." She looked at me critically. "Well, you were."

"Trish," said Gary.

"Of course, you meet all types at uni," Trish continued. I hadn't realised she was at university.

"What are you studying?" I asked. But perhaps that was indelicate. Mother said she had been *sent away,* as if disgrace was attached to it. I tried not to think too closely of what my mother would say about this adventure. Imagined words fluttered against my mind.

"Teaching, surprisingly enough," supplied Gary. "She missed so much the first time around."

Trish hit him, and the truck swerved. I held on.

"Is that . . . wise?" I asked gingerly, glancing at Trish's unlit cigarette, her tattoo. "Are you a . . ." I faltered. She had a piercing in her nose. I hadn't noticed that before. "A good example?"

Gary cleared his throat but didn't look at me. Trish did nothing but stare. The truck shook over rough road, and Trish blurred at the edges; I looked away.

"What the hell is wrong with you, Tina?" she demanded. "Did you hit your head? Or have you been brainwashed or something? No, back off, Gary. Tina, you're wearing a *dress* and a bloody *pastel cardigan*." She swore again and I winced.

"Quit it," said Gary.

"No. No, you quit it, Gary. Because if you could have stopped this, believe I'm going to blame you. Pull over. Let me drive. I'm creeped out, sitting next to her."

"No," said Gary calmly. How far was it to Carter's Crossing? Had we gone too far to turn back?

I risked a glance at Trish, who was watching me as if I were a snake coiled beside her.

"It was time to grow up, Patricia," I said quietly. "My mother needed me."

"Like. Hell."

"Trish, you haven't been here," said Gary.

"*You* have, and look what happened. Tina, what did she do to you?"

"Nothing! I *stayed*. Everyone else left." *You want to be with me, don't you, Bettina?* I couldn't imagine anywhere I'd rather be. I hadn't imagined anywhere else at all. To be so far from Runagate already frightened me like falling.

"Let's kidnap her," said Trish. "We can just keep driving." Her voice was brassy. "We'll get to the coast eventually. Go to my place and hide out there. We're between housemates. We can give her a makeover."

"You remember what my grandmother says about waking sleepwalkers—" said Gary.

"No, no, I don't. It's probably something awful. But this— for once, this really *isn't* natural, Gary. Tina, you were my best friend." She was remembering wrong. She was thinking of someone else. "You were a terrible influence. It's been—what? Three years? And you stay home and bake patty-cakes?"

Gary was driving faster, not watching us. Looking at the mirror.

"I went to the botanic gardens just before I came back here," said Trish. "They have a building full of bonsai trees. Stunted. Horrible. Don't know why I thought of that."

"My mother loves me," I said.

"She loves what she's made you, maybe," said Trish.

"What do you know about it, anyway, Trish?" asked Gary.

"More than you, evidently!" said Trish. "Or I care more. I haven't seen one thing about this—this china doll here to prove she's our Tina."

"She's run away," Gary pointed out. "She's dragged us with her."

"'You will help me, won't you, Gary Damson?'" mimicked Trish unpleasantly. "And here you are."

"And here we are," he agreed. He hadn't mentioned that I threw paint at his car.

"Let's just *keep* driving," said Trish. "We'll call from a truck stop and explain. But we won't go back."

"No!" I said. The road, the sliding planes of trees and light were bad enough. Endless echoes of what had been at the edge of my sight for so long. But at least this road, these fences anchored us to Runagate. To go further *would* be running away. This had been a mistake. Everything I had taught myself to be, all my mother's lessons, snapped back. I scrabbled at the door handle. "You can't make me. I didn't want to leave. I just wanted to know—" Know what, I didn't remember. I needed to be free of the rush and closeness, the rattling and noise.

Trish grabbed me around the shoulders. "Stop, Gary! She's going to jump!"

Gary braked. Trish, still holding me, slid forward and banged her elbow into the dashboard. She didn't let go.

But I wasn't the reason Gary had stopped. Sergeant Aberdeen was pulling up behind us. I'd never even seen his lights flashing. He came over and leaned on Gary's window.

"Young Mr Damson. Do you have a working seatbelt in that deathtrap yet?"

"Trish is doing double duty, sir," said Gary.

Sergeant Aberdeen looked further in. I was too mortified to struggle.

"Hey, Dad," said Trish. "We're kidnapping Tina." But she let me go. I straightened my dress and ran my fingers through my hair, trying to look meek and respectable. My neck hurt, an old ache, and the rhythm of the wheels still rattled in my joints. I wanted to be on the sturdy earth.

"Sergeant Aberdeen," I said.

"Hello, Miss Scott," he said gravely. *My mother has woken up,* I thought, taking refuge in panic, a cocoon of fears. *She found me missing and told the police. She will be frantic with worry, and disappointed. I am a terrible daughter. Maybe the*

house caught fire and she ran to safety and doesn't think I sur-
vived. I am—

"Patricia," he said. "You could have left a note."

"You could have let me get a mobile phone."

"They don't work out here," said Sergeant Aberdeen. He looked back at me. "It's been a long time since I've had to threaten to detain you. These two are Known To The Police. Are you with them willingly?"

We liked Winston Aberdeen, my mother said. He had been good to us. It took me a moment to realise he was laughing at me.

"It was her idea," said Gary.

"Bettina Scott," said Sergeant Aberdeen gently, talking past Gary. "I can take you back to town."

I hesitated. My bones felt weak; I had been afraid and sick since we left Runagate. And yet—

"Da-ad," said Trish.

"She's looking for her brothers," said Gary. "We thought she ought to."

Sergeant Aberdeen's smile faded. He glanced at Trish.

"Wasn't my idea," said Trish. "I'm over it."

"Sir," said Gary. "What really happened to Mr Scott? And the boys?"

Sergeant Aberdeen just shook his head. "I don't indulge idle gossip," he said.

"Maybe if you did, they'd have turned up!" said Trish sharply. But Sergeant Aberdeen looked tired and sad. Trish's mother had disappeared too, I remembered. But that was a mystery: nothing like my family.

"My father just *left*, Patricia," I said. My voice felt small. "People do that, don't they?"

"They-found-your-dad's-car-in-the-gully," said Trish in a rush. "There was a murder investigation—"

"Trish—"

"Shut up, Gary! Tina, how can you not know this?"

"Because it isn't true," I said. "Mother reported him as missing, but he didn't want to be found."

Trish swore. I tried to ignore it. Gary frowned. Sergeant Aberdeen looked at me like he hadn't really seen me before.

"Well, kiddo?" he said at last. "It looks like it's been a big day. Let's take you back." He'd take me home and everything would be as it was. But I wasn't a kid.

"I will go," I said, truthfully, and then, although it hurt as much as anything I'd ever done, as if I were pulling my heart out by the roots, "but not yet."

My mother would have spoken softly to him, to me, and it would have been easy to do the right thing. But she wasn't there. He nodded, stepped away and slapped the side of the truck. I turned to look through the rear window, watching the pattern of blue and white checks vanish behind its own dust. He would tell my mother. I got out.

"What now?" exploded Trish. I couldn't explain. I needed to stand for a moment on the same earth my mother stood on.

"We could all stretch our legs," said Gary, opening his door. "Clear your head, Trish."

"*My* head?" said Trish.

"Put a sock in it," said Gary wearily. "Mrs Scott was probably trying to protect her."

"From what?" said Trish, although I heard her slide across the seat. "You don't believe that. It's not what she said to my dad. I bet it's not what she said to you. I'm sure as hell you've got your own reasons for being here, Gary Damson."

I cleared my throat and scuffed one shoe through the white dirt. "What did my mother say?"

"She said you were unbalanced, she was trying to keep you quiet and help you to recover, family life recently had been distressing for you—she didn't want you to be overstimulated," said Trish, in a mincing echo of my mother's voice. "She was afraid you were an unsettling influence on me, and while your, uh, *violent tendencies* were just a stage—acting out—she wouldn't want me to get drawn into that spiral. She said she had hopes for your recovery. I guess it worked," she finished bitterly.

There was a murder investigation. No, he couldn't be dead. They hadn't found a body. I touched my collarbone and felt my heartbeat. Would I *know* if he had died?

"I would never be violent," I said.

You must not be so . . . helter-skelter, said my mother. *Remember—you are calm and dignified. Remember. Remember. Yes, Mother.* I recollected myself and stopped ruining my shoe.

"You weren't violent," said Trish. "That was Mitch and Chris. You have—had—a violent mind. Impulsive. You never had a good idea, but you could make anything sound like one. Dad hated it. I think he was glad to send me to boarding school. Anyway, we wrote, Gary and I, when you wouldn't talk to us, but your mother told us not to. And you never bothered to answer."

I didn't believe her, and yet I could imagine the conversations, after the letters had arrived, with Sergeant Aberdeen—since Trish was away—and Gary. Mother gentle, slightly sad. *That was just a little thoughtless, wasn't it, Gary dear, to bring this all up again? Just a trifle unkind?* Waiting until Gary mumbled, *Yes, Mrs Scott.*

I kicked at the dirt, viciously. I hadn't wanted this. I just wanted to know if my brothers had sent the letter.

Trish had jumped up to sit on the bonnet of the truck and lit her cigarette. "Why act like it's such a big deal, like no-one's ever asked questions around here? It's what my dad *does*. Why do you think he's stayed in Runagate? Last time my mum was ever seen was somewhere in Inglewell. He should leave; we should all go."

"Unfinished business," said Gary.

"I don't believe in ghosts."

"You believed in the megarrity right enough."

"Only because I saw—"

They bickered on. I ought to have hated the sound, but it fell easily into the background. I climbed the rough verge of the road to the fence. Flowers like puffed rice scraped my hem, loose dirt and grey leaves gave beneath my feet, sifted through my sandals. A small shelter rusted there—a stand for milk cans, or perhaps a mailbox, now empty except for leaves and fine-limbed spiders. The tin, lovely in decay, curved hot under my hand. Peace.

"You'll get tetanus," called Trish. "I'm not explaining that to your mother. Tell her, Gary."

There might be dozens of places like this. The shelter was right beside the road, and I hadn't seen it. Whole buildings could sink into the trees and disappear. How much easier for people to vanish.

Hot wind vibrated in the fence wires, flickered the light through the branches. "Come on," said Gary, and opened his door. "Let's keep moving."

"How much *farther*?" groaned Trish. "There aren't even any decent radio stations out here."

"I'll tell you a worse story than 'The Megarrity' if you'll shut up for a bit!" said Gary.

Trish said something awful, but back inside the truck I was happy not to talk. Although it was poor posture, I leaned against the door, letting the jolts jar my teeth, and watched the blur of the road, listening to Gary Damson. Even later, after everything, when I tried to piece together the tale, I was never sure how much of it he intended to be true.

THE SAWMILL

Once there was a boy called . . .

"Gary?" suggested Trish.

Let's say he was called Jack. Boys in fairy tales always are. Twelve years old and too small for it. Certain the world was withholding something. Burned to freckles except for his feet inside his boots and his skinny chest beneath his shirt, pale as a fish belly. His dad was a contractor—they moved about, but he had lived around Inglewell all his life, and if he'd paid more attention to the stories he'd heard, he'd have known better.

His old uncle—well, not precisely an uncle, but a cousin of

sorts—knocked on the door of the caravan one day (this was just before Jack's mum inherited some land). "Jack," he said, furtively. "I've got a job for you."

Jack's mother would have asked, "Davy Spicer, is this something dangerous?" Although she was born a Spicer, she didn't approve of Uncle Davy. But she was working at the library— there used to be one at Carter's Crossing on Tuesdays—so Jack asked, "How much?"

"As much as you're worth," said his uncle. "Get down here."

I—*Jack* jumped into the long grass around the caravan. His uncle cuffed the back of his head, not quite affectionately, and they climbed into Uncle Davy's low-slung Holden Kingswood WB. The best ute in the world.

It was a long drive, but where isn't? They went by back roads and across paddocks. Jack climbed up and down, opening sagging wire gates. His uncle said, "Just leave them. They're no friends of ours." But Jack knew that much about the world—he levered each one closed again.

They ran out of tracks. Wattle saplings whipped the ute's bullbar, dragged under and sprang up again. Then Uncle Davy stopped at a fence, properly built, with a metal gate in it. On the other side, tangled with glittering box and old ironbark, was a crowd of cypress pines, dark save for the blue-green buds of their pinecones. There was a dent in the trees that might have been the start of a track.

"Get on with it," said his uncle.

Jack dropped into the wire-grass and waded to the gate. It was tall as he was, latched with a chain and a metal hook, rusted tight but not locked. He had to shoulder it open against the clawing cotton bush, bracing into the bars and pushing with his legs straight. His uncle drove through, and Jack closed it again, fumbling with the chain.

The cypress pines pressed pungent against the windows and shrieked over the top of the ute, hissing and rattling along the tray. Once, Jack and his uncle had to drag a fallen tree clear of their path. Then the way opened into weeds and cotton bush. They were at the end of the track. Jack's uncle killed the engine.

In front of them, there had once been several small huts. Their timbers were grey and splintered, corrugated roofs corroded and folded in, porches sagging. A shed had collapsed over flakes of orange rust.

"What is it?" asked Jack.

"Sawmill," said his uncle. "Was." He gestured to a length of track. An iron trolley propped up one end of the fallen roof.

"What are we going to do?"

His uncle pointed toward the third hut. "You," he said, "are going in there to fetch out what you find."

"Why me?" said Jack.

"Because you're a skinny runt and the floors are rotten," said his uncle. "There'll be a box of old glass bottles." He tossed his pocket knife to Jack. "Make it snappy. I'll be waiting."

The steps creaked and cracked. Something rustled hurriedly under them.

"Get on with it!" said my uncle.

*"His *uncle*," corrected Trish.*

He isn't close family, Jack reminded himself. Probably there were snakes in the hut. Definitely below it. The splintered boards of the narrow porch gaped under his boots; when he grabbed one of the posts, the roof shifted. His uncle laughed—a sharp bark. Jack, straightening, trod carefully where nails bled rust onto the planks, and hoped the beams were solid.

The door hung at an angle from a hinge of riveted leather. The lower one had been gnawed through. Jack eased it open and edged into the hut.

The darkness surprised him. Hot slivers of blue sky were bright through gaps in the roof, and blades of shining dust floated between the boards over the window, but even with the door ajar, the light didn't get far.

"Well?" called his uncle. "Can you see it?"

"It's dark!" shouted Jack. The ceiling creaked like footsteps. He lowered his voice and hissed over his shoulder, "I can't see." Air brushed his face. Air, or spiders.

He heard his uncle tramping through the grass. Jack, just inside the door, waited for his eyes to adjust. Slumped shadows, cushions hanging heavy with rot. Oddly, he could not smell mice. Only mouldy cloth, dry wood and beneath that a stale draft rising through the floorboards, damply cold on his shins.

Weren't there stories about sinkholes, and caves? He shifted his foot. Something light sifted between the planks: splinters, perhaps, or leaves. He didn't hear it hit anything.

Even if the ground was only half a metre beneath him, he wouldn't hear a leaf hit it. But the possibility that the ground was—just maybe—far, far more than a metre away kept him motionless until his uncle tramped back and rolled a torch across the porch and through the door. It drummed on the floor, loud as the beating of Jack's heart in his ears.

"I want to come out," Jack said.

"Get the bottles first," said his uncle.

Jack turned, but his uncle had stepped onto the porch. He

pushed the door shut, and Jack couldn't find a handle. He hammered on the timber.

"I should have known Marilyn's son would be a coward," said his uncle. "Shut that racket or you'll bring the whole place down." Something slid off the roof and crashed into the grass. Jack found the torch and switched it on.

He was in a small, square room crowded with discarded boxes. The closest were cardboard; their corners had swollen and split, spilling toys onto the floor—faded plastic trucks and bald baby dolls with naked cotton bodies. They smelled bad and shivered in the torchlight.

Jack edged his way between them into the centre of the hut. Why was this stuff so important, anyway? It wasn't antiques. Just trash someone hadn't bothered taking to the tip. With the knife, he levered open a lid. Only paper gnawed to lace. Silverfish scattered, grey in the light. *VISIT THE SUN-SHINE* read part of a yellowed newspaper on a flattish parcel. Jack prodded it. A plate.

A sagging narrow mattress, badly stained. Boxes labelled in marker that had run in brownish-purple streaks. TAX + RAIN GAUGE said one, but only had empty photo albums in it. Another read DRESS UPS. Masking tape peeled off the cardboard like bark. Three hollow-sided vinyl suitcases. Tools: fence strainers and old saws, which he understood, and others he didn't. The saw was still sharp: he touched it and brought away a bead of blood on his hand. "What about tetanus?" his mother would say. "Did you even think about tetanus?" He sucked at the cut.

"Jack!"

"I'm looking!"

But there, on the far side of the room, on a rickety rocking chair, its legs held together with twisted cord, was a box of bottles.

They were not beer bottles or Coke bottles or even wine flagons. They were all much smaller and much older. Their edges were blurred and their sides were milky. Green and amber and deep midnight blue, with INK or POISON or names pressing up out of the glass itself.

"I've found it!" said Jack.

The bottom of the box sagged dangerously. He had to balance the torch on top of the bottles, under his chin. The floor was a pool of shadow. He couldn't see if he was stepping on top of the beams.

"Hurry up!" called Uncle Davy. Although there were cracks in the walls and door, he sounded a long way away.

"I am," grated Jack. Then a floorboard broke and his foot went through.

Maybe he didn't hear the board fall because it hit the ground when the box hit the floor, and maybe it just kept falling. Short as he was, the hut wasn't *that* high. He should have touched dirt with the toe of his boot, but it swung loose, and his leg was caught between the planks well above his knee.

Jack's heart was beating so loud, he couldn't hear his uncle. He could barely hear the clatter of bottles rolling around him. His only thought was to get his leg clear of—whatever was beneath the house.

When he was free and could breathe again, Jack looked for the bottles. They were small enough and had spilled low enough that most were unbroken. He swept them together, away from the cold velvet space in the floor. The bottom of the box had torn through, so he pulled off his shirt and filled that. Then he reached for the torch. It rolled from his hand, flickering, tilted a moment on the edge of the hole, and fell. It spun down into blackness, flashing as it twisted. Then it struck something and the light stopped, but the echoes kept going. Like a heartbeat.

Jack was cold with sweat. He scrambled through the dark, felt for his shirt, knocked a small, hard thing that rolled— another bottle—grabbed that too and backed away from the broken floor. He groped his way to the mouldering mattress, climbed it and pulled at the boards over the window. They came loose almost at once.

The sky was so bright, it stung tears into Jack's eyes. The dark pines were glowing red smudges; his uncle was a skeletal shadow. "You'd be late for your own funeral," said Uncle Davy. "Where's the box?"

"It broke," said Jack. He held the clanking bundle of his shirt down. "The floor broke. I dropped the torch." His leg throbbed dully. "I think I cut myself."

"Idiot," said Uncle Davy, turning back toward the ute. He had taken the shirt full of bottles, and his pocket knife.

Jack crouched on top of the mattress, judging the distance from the window to the ground. The front of his leg was cold; when he touched it, his hand came away red. He heard the ute's engine start.

"Wait!" he shouted, his fear of crossing the floor of the hut evaporating. "Wait for me!"

He jumped.

He landed on hands and feet, jarring all his joints, and sprawled a moment in the hot sand, glad to feel the sun on his back. No dark at all; no dank chill. But Uncle Davy had turned the ute.

Jack leaped up and galloped after it, hopping at times to spare his leg. But the ute pulled out in a shower of leaves, as if something swifter than a limping boy was after it. It pushed into the broken trees and roared off.

At the edge of the pines, where the air was sticky with the smell of resin, Jack bent, gasping for air, then turned. The light was golden around the sawmill. He half-expected the buildings to have fallen into the earth, but they squatted, broken and unwelcoming. His leg hurt; sand caked the seeping blood, and one foot was bare. His chest was bruised, and his leg too. He rubbed it and felt the bottle still in his pocket.

In the warm light, the glass was dull. But it wasn't empty. It had a chalky-silver lid, and when he shook it next to his ear, it made a sandy whisper. It had words on it, too, like the POISON bottles, but this one said FARRIER-something. Part of a paper label clung to it: *OOD FOR BEAST AND MA*. On the other side of the bottle was a lump in the glass: a skull and crossbones. Even better than POISON. Not *FOOD FOR BEAST*, then. He'd take it to school. Even the teachers would be interested. The historical house might want it. Maybe it would be valuable, and Mr Alleman would interview him for the *STAR*.

Jack squatted on his heels in the sparse, sharp grass near the trees, waiting for his uncle to return. Evening was arriving. The light grew richer, the trees behind him darker. It would be smart to stay at the sawmill, but he didn't want to be near that deep black emptiness.

Long leaves trailed over Jack's bare shoulders as he limped down the track, like spiders and ticks crawling over him, however much he tried to shrug the feeling off. Branches cracked in the twig-misted depths of the overgrown pine plantation, then a roo drummed the ground, and it was silent again.

Jack fidgeted with the bottle, warm beneath his fingers. Maybe no one remembered the sawmill was there, and no one would look for him. But there had to be a real road nearby. Once, trucks would have carted the timber away. Or maybe his uncle was waiting at the gate, laughing.

Jack pulled out the bottle. Its contents glittered and shifted like dust. Gold dust. Water would be more use. He wondered how long it would take him to walk home. If it was gold, maybe they could settle near town. Live in a real house, like his grandparents, although theirs was in Woodwild, practically a ghost town. Like Uncle Davy, although his was the old Spicer place.

Jack opened the bottle.

It wasn't gold. It rose, glittering like bubbles in lemonade. Up into the thin bars of evening sun, slow and deliberate. Jack clapped his hand over the bottle; instantly, the stuff puffed up like flour. It scratched in his throat and lungs and brain.

When he stopped sneezing, the air was clear except for the haze of dusk. A little dust remained in the bottle. Jack screwed the lid back and put the bottle in his pocket. He did not feel sick, but he heard the drumming again: his heart thundering, the blood in his ears like marching feet and, along his spine, a certainty of deep, cold darkness under the earth. He spun around. Nothing but trees and, nearby, the sawmill. Night hurried through the pines.

Limping on, Jack tried to think of anything but darkness. Instead, he thought of the glittering dust, the prickling in the back of his mind. Of gold and the wishes it would have made come true. Of the books his mum brought home from the library, the stories his grandmother told, strange bottles and wishes.

"I wish," he began. Something, startled, crashed through the trees.

"I wish," he said loudly, "that we had a real house. With

bookcases for Mum," he amended quickly. Jack's uncle had a fancy old bookcase that locked, full of outdated almanacs, Reader's Digest Condensed Books and older volumes turned backs-to-the-wall with marbling on the edges of their pages. Library books, wrapped in plastic fastened with yellowing sticky-tape, smelled peculiar.

The sky was gold, then pink, then pale as new wood, but among the trees night already curled around him like smoke. Jack walked as loudly as he could, missing one boot, to frighten off anything in the shadows. He was twelve, and small as he was, there wasn't anything bigger than him in the trees that hadn't been brought from England. But his grandmother told him terrible things and his mum had read him *The Hound of the Baskervilles* once; he'd never been entirely comfortable with the night since, especially when he heard—he paused on one foot to pick bindies from the bare one and listened. Nothing howled. Nothing at all.

"I wish!" he said loudly, and paused. He was going to say, *I wish my friends were here,* but he didn't have many. The bottle might fix that. So would having a real house. So he wished for friends, mumbling it in case something in the trees laughed at him, or his uncle, waiting nearby, heard.

Jack thought hard about the third wish. Wishing for a million dollars never ended well in books, and this might be his last wish, if he got any at all. He could wish for a truck of his own and leave this awful place. But the fun of thinking about wishes had worn off. He was almost sick with tiredness and fury and the lingering fright of falling. Mostly, although he wasn't sure later whether he said it aloud or if that even mattered, he wished his uncle could get as big a fright as he had. Or worse.

Jack fought his way out of the cypress forest. The air was

silver-grey, and he heaved himself over the old gate to stagger in the sharp, night-bright grass on the other side. His bare foot was sore, the climb had broken up the scabbing blood on his leg, and his mum would be worrying. Jack tried not to feel sorry for himself. He'd heard Old Pinnicke, when he was young, had been rolled on by a horse and dragged himself through the bush for three days until he found help. "Never been the same since, of course," the story had ended, which was hardly comforting. Besides, Jack couldn't imagine Old Pinnicke ever having been young.

Odd, he realised belatedly, that after all Uncle Davy's complaining, his uncle had paused to shut the gate.

Ahead, faint in the moonlight, were two fading lines where the ute's tyres had brought them across the paddock. He could track them back, he'd read about trackers, or . . . He looked down at the dirt, and along the fence on each side. There had been a firebreak there once, wide as a track, although it hadn't been kept up—the fencer in Jack disapproved—and he could see a broken bush where his uncle must have turned the ute aside, leaving. That would be the way to the road.

Pleased with himself, Jack jog-limped along, ignoring the sounds of the night, which seemed louder there than they had in the pines. Just the wind hissing in the grass, birds shifting in the saplings, pademelons leaving their tussocks for the night. A distant thumping—trucks on a rough road, or a pump. Not his heart—too metallic.

He would have missed Davy Spicer's ute if it weren't for the smell of oil and rubber acrid on the cool breeze. It had plunged into a dip on the side of the track, among the trees; fence wires, loose around it, hummed on the air.

Jack stood on one foot for a long time. The engine pinged under the hood, and metal scraped like fingernails. Unbreathing, he edged up to the ute. Its windscreen was white with starred glass and moonlight.

He was glad he hadn't wished for a truck.

The driver's door was open but the passenger door, closest to Jack, was closed. The darkness in the cab was like the darkness in the hut. *Just walk on, Jack!* his nerves screamed.

He got his fingers under the handle and lifted it. The door was downhill, and a weight pushed from inside. The truck creaked.

I could have wished for him to be alive, thought Jack. The door pulled free from his hand. His uncle must have been leaning against it for, bloodied and staring as if he'd had a far, far worse fright than Jack had, Davy Spicer's body fell limply sideways.

Jack ran.

CHAPTER FOUR

EVER ON

"Oh, piss off!" said Trish.

"Look in the glovebox," said Gary.

Trish stared at him then, leaning across me, jerked the glovebox open. Wire cutters, tins and maps fell onto my sandals, leaving a black mark on the white straps. Trish rummaged and at last brought out a small bottle, milky with age. She pulled a face and shook the bottle. Below the thunder of the wheels, we heard a faint drumming. I felt queasy. Gary looked innocent.

"Knock it off, Damson!" said Trish. Gary's fingers stopped their movement, fanned above the steering wheel. Lines sprang from the corners of his eyes. He was laughing.

"Idiot," said Trish, and feinted at him. I shut my eyes.

Night and crumpled metal, bleeding petrol and the hiss of the breeze in broken wire, fading headlights as my father wades with the only torch into the night, forever.

"Ill-gotten wishes *are* the only reason you have friends," said Trish. "God, you're superstitious."

"You're the one who jumped!"

I opened my eyes. The dream, or memory, evaporated. We were still on the road, rattling across a timber bridge. A feeling of greenery below the sand. One Eye Man Creek, said the sign.

Trish squinted at the translucent glass. The tattooed wolf— attenuated, unreal—stretched and shifted with her shoulder.

"Some of these things are worth a lot," she said. "We should find that sawmill. I've seen them in antique stores: old phones, bottles. You'd be surprised what people have in their sheds."

Gary glanced sideways at me. Once as if he had asked a question I hadn't heard, the second time as if he was worried.

"Are you okay?" he said.

"A headache," I said faintly, although that wasn't true. I wasn't sure what hurt, or even if it was pain. But headaches were ladylike lies. I closed my eyes and rested my head on the shabby headrest, keeping my hands clasped and elbows in, away from Trish, who sprawled beside me. I wanted to think but wasn't sure how.

Trish snorted. "Was there a point to that story, Gary?"

"No. Except— There wasn't a body when we went back. It always seemed like a coincidence: Uncle Davy, then Mr Scott. *Two* men disappearing, both vanished from the wrecks of crashed cars . . . I've got questions too." But he didn't say for whom.

We reached Carter's Crossing, and the brief hiss of bitumen, by lunchtime. I dropped from the cab gladly. *We don't travel well, do we, Bettina?* I would have sat on the ground, but Trish grabbed my arm as if she thought I was going to fall.

"I'm quite well," I said, disengaging myself. "Thank you." When we walked, I stayed carefully out of reach.

Carter's Crossing was the smallest of the three towns of Inglewell. One street, a few houses leaning and fading into encroaching trees. A roofless grey building that might have been a church. Not even a closed railway station: the line went right by. The only shop was a shed labelled CROSSING MOTORS. Its roller door was almost all the way down.

"Stay here," said Gary. "She knows me. Well, she knows you two, too. Just . . . stay back."

We lingered near the kerb while Gary crouched to talk under the door.

"You wouldn't have stood for that, once," said Trish.

"Margie—hey, Miss Hale?" Gary was saying. "I'm trying to find a bloke in a ute. Beardy. Taller—well, taller than me. Has a mate with him. Old Holden?" he said, and looked back at me as if I would have noticed, but I only remembered the geese. "It was in bad shape. Cages on the back. Your sister said—no, Casey—said they were from out this way?" He waited.

Trish and I, standing back, couldn't hear the answer.

"You never used to let anyone speak for you," Trish went on. "Especially Gary."

"He just wants to help."

"Why's that, do you think?" asked Trish, nastily.

I didn't know. *We don't associate with the Damsons.* But I hadn't had to beg Gary to help look for my brothers—he'd arrived almost as soon as I sent word through Trish. Thinking about reasons was uncomfortable.

"He knew Mitch and Chris," I said distantly. The word

friends stirred in my memory. But my brothers had been wild and uncivilised—my mother said so, and I agreed—and *friends* was such a petty word. "Maybe they . . . owed him money?" Trish looked at me sideways, sighed.

"Margie Hale's mad as a cut snake," she said. "Once, she chased Chris and me clear into the bush—remember how light-footed Chris was? But we only lost her by pretending to be the bone horse, clattering in the trees, until we freaked ourselves out. Almost didn't find our way back to the road. Chris said he *did* see something, but I bet it was a wild dog. Or a pig." For a moment, she had relaxed, but now her face tightened. The trees bent over Carter's Crossing; the town had fallen asleep and would never wake again.

"What did you *do* to her?" I asked. Trish shook herself and went on.

"*You'd* said Old Pinnicke told you—he'd say anything; he was ranting about traps this morning—there was a grave-yard behind the shed where she buried her husbands," she said, with pleasant reminiscence. "We were going to dig up a skull—and get a look at Margie Hale while we were at it. Even that was your fault." She sniffed. "I'm surprised the boys weren't *more* irritated by you."

Too many questions. I retreated to the certainty of my mother's lessons: *We neither dignify nor indulge vulgar curiosity, do we, Bettina?*

"Surely, you know I wouldn't tell such a tale, don't you, Patricia?" I said at last, gently as my mother.

Trish opened her mouth, closed it, shrugged uncomfortably—I thrilled with the triumph of being on firmer ground.

"Don't answer her," said Gary, returning to stand between us. He gave me a quick narrow glance before going on. I looked over him at Trish and felt a disconcerting familiarity. *Gary Damson puffed up proud as a bantam between the two of you.* Whose voice had that been? Not my mother's.

Gary was still talking. "She said a couple of rough bushies stop by occasionally; the man you saw—or someone like him. But if he wanted supplies she couldn't order or hold, they might have gone to Casey in Runagate to collect them. They come in from further west. And I said we'd deliver Gwenda Sage's mail." He waved a slightly dirty package of envelopes, rolled into the same home catalogue my mother subscribed to.

"Sage?" I said, tilting my head to see the cover: lamps with beaded fringes. My mother would like those. "Like the postmaster?"

"Mr Sage's sister," said Gary. "I don't think they're on speaking terms."

"We aren't running *errands,*" said Trish.

"It's the cost of info from Margie," said Gary, shamefacedly. "They don't get on. She said Gwenda likes to keep an eye on comings and goings. She could know more, but you might have to talk to her, Trish; she doesn't have much time for . . . my sort."

"What? Fencers?" said Trish. "At least you've got a job." We trudged back to the truck. As we climbed in, I saw a featureless oval look through the mesh glass of the Crossing Motors' one window. It didn't move until we were gone. "Feckless youths?"

"Damsons," said Gary.

"Did *they* have names?" I surprised myself by asking. My face grew hot; I wished for my mother's cool, flower-scented hands. *Clever questions only display ignorance, don't they? Yes, Mother.* "The man? For deliveries?"

"Smith," said Gary shortly.

"You realise this is a wild goose chase?" said Trish.

I followed them to the truck. The ground felt foreign, and my feet heavy on it.

The sun sailed inexorably across the sky. As we crossed each creek and bridge, something stretched tighter than wire below my ribs.

"It won't be them," Trish said. "The boys, I mean."

I hadn't said it was. *We thought she ought to look.* I hadn't thought Gary might know more than I did.

"Trish," said Gary, thoughtfully, "did Nerida—Mrs Scott—know you were with us all, that last time?"

"She made a point about it. Came and talked to me over the fence, nastily polite. Said she knew I'd been running about and, oh, that I was . . . never the decorous one, was I? I think she suspected about me and . . . Well."

Gary snorted. I sniffed.

"She was laughing at me," said Trish. "She said Tina had been home in bed like a good girl and Tina was there agreeing and—"

Gary braked, swerved and stopped.

"SHIT!" said Trish, bracing herself.

A swift long shadow dissolved into the scrub beside the road. My ears were ringing; the old ache in my neck was back. I put my hand to my cheek and the faint thread of my old scar.

"What was that?" said Trish.

"Nothing," said Gary. He was pale. "A feral dog. Mangy. Long gone."

"No dog I ever saw," muttered Trish, and shuddered. Gary

drove on. I craned out the window but saw nothing. *Foolishness,* my mother said. Those stories about half-glimpsed creatures in the hills.

"Where *was* Tina that night?" Gary continued. That last night. The night my father left.

"What is this? The inquisition?" said Trish. "Dad's right, by the way. You need seatbelts. *Betty* here was home being a wet blanket."

Gary raised his eyebrows. "Whose idea was it to go up the water tower?"

"Intense much, Damson?" said Trish. "Everyone goes up the water tower."

"No, they don't. Just bloody-minded Scotts with firecrackers. You know she was the worst of them."

They might have been talking about a dead girl. *Water warm as blood, and below that, cold as stars.* I would have said I couldn't even swim, yet memories surfaced, sluggish and drowned.

"What did she do?" said Trish, scathing. "Shout directions from her bedroom window?"

"Who got the car and decided on blind tag that night?" said Gary.

Driving only by moonlight, the pale night sky blazing.

"I was at home, asleep," I said, holding to what I knew was true. "Wasn't I?"

Trish opened her mouth to answer. Gary said to me, "Don't, Tina. Trish?"

Trish turned to look at me, then back to Gary. "She was with us," she said slowly. "With you and me and Chris and

Mitch." She rounded on me, furious, as if it were my fault she—we—had forgotten. She spoke quickly. "You were there the whole time! It was your *idea*. You got us in trouble, and you didn't get blamed at all! It wasn't fair! Then your dad disappeared, so everyone was sorry for you and no one wanted to dob you in. Shit. Gary. How did I forget?"

Strong emotions were unbecoming. Unsettling.

"The Scotts are persuasive," said Gary.

"Why do *you* remember?" she asked him.

He shrugged, worked up through the gears as we got on our way again. "Practice. And Tina didn't talk to me at all. But I'm glad you remember. I was starting to think *I* was the crazy one."

Trish crossed her arms. My mind choked with leaves and dust and distance, the slow unravelling of certainties. I missed sitting empty under the lemon tree, thinking only of the lace of the pepperina, the dance of Mr Alleman's lantern-bush.

"*She* was with *us*," she repeated, and looked at me. "For a while there, people thought you did it, Tina."

So many questions, but I knew she was waiting for me to ask another. Reluctant, I said, "What did they think I'd done?"

"Trish," said Gary, wearily.

"Killed your dad," said Trish.

There weren't many appropriate replies to that. Trish watched me. Gary drove on beneath a tunnel of arching branches, the sun spangling down on the blue-patched bitumen.

There must be some deep aquifer of emotion I could not

tap. I couldn't have killed my father—a lady *doesn't*. Had I known I was suspected of it? Closing my eyes, I felt gingerly among these stirred-up memories, not wanting to discover too much. Mother must have protected me. But Mitch and Chris would know what had happened.

Gary swore. I opened my eyes. He reversed off the broken shoulder, turned us around and went back until he found a road he'd overshot. The bitumen gave way once more to red pebbles and white dust, but rougher here, and the paddocks between the trees were overgrown, shaggy with silver grass, laced with wandering creek beds.

A single low old telephone wire from tree to tree beside the road; the shadow of the truck flickered along the raised bank of the verge. Keeping pace.

"Mr Scott found me, after the crash," said Gary at last.

"You mean he found 'Jack'," said Trish, half-heartedly.

"That battered old station wagon, grinding along the road. I don't know what he was doing there. He picked me up in the headlights. I didn't think he was going to stop at first. When he got the story straight, we drove through the paddock to the wreck. He parked with his lights full on it. I remember him in stained jeans and a torn shirt. All I could think was *stained and torn by what?* I didn't know what he did for a living.

"I sat in the passenger seat and shivered in the dark. I remember wishing he hadn't left his door open."

"Bad things happen just as much by day, Dad says," said Trish. "Especially out here."

At least at night, I thought, you know why you can't quite see the things you glimpse from the corner of your eye. At least you can't see the trees. I barely remembered my father's face now. Why could I see him so vividly when Gary described him? It was as if the boundaries of memory had been moved.

"Mitch and Chris were big and loud even then, but Mr Scott wasn't—still, he waded away with a torch like he wasn't scared of anything. I wanted to warn him about the drumming I'd heard, like hooves. I was thinking of the stories of the bone horse and the megarrity, and all those animals people see but never catch. Then a hand touched mine and I yelled."

Trish, listening more than she pretended to, swore.

"It was Tina," Gary said. "She was in the back seat. 'It'll be all right,' she said. Mum didn't like me taking the school bus when Mitch and Chris were on it—I wasn't meant to hang around the Scott kids. It had never been a problem; we hadn't exactly been friends. But wild Tina Scott said, quite calm, 'It'll be all right. Dad'll fix it.'"

The strange Damson boy, shivering in the passenger seat, his bare shoulder bony in the faint back-glow of the headlights. But that would have been a long way from Runagate, and I was a town girl.

"Did he?" said Trish.

Gary shook his head. "He said there wasn't anything there. Maybe Uncle Davy had just been stunned. Maybe he'd dragged himself into the bush. I don't know. They never found anything. Not even the other bottles."

I remembered the feeling of the upholstery under my hand, the *clunk* of the door-latches, the sag of the ceiling lining tented around the light. My father—*Dad*—pocketing a knife as he slid back into the driver's seat.

"You are the *worst*, Gary Damson," said Trish. "Why are you only telling us all this now?"

"Just making conversation," said Gary. "We're here."

Trish elbowed me. "Gate."

The long, stiff grass at the base of the gatepost and around the fresh-painted blue mail stand plucked at my dress with tiny claws; the air under the sleek-barked gums felt oily. The gate was newer than the fence; its latch was a half-moon of bent metal hooked over the top bar. It resisted, although it didn't look secure. Only when I pulled the gate closed after the truck did I see the skull in the hollow of the post. A small skull, beaked, perfectly sized to fit a cupped palm.

I was partly horrified, part fascinated. I knew how smooth the bone would be, frail in the sunshine as lemon flowers. *Dreadful morbidity,* my mother had said, as I threw the basket of bones and snakeskin onto the fire she'd had me build at the back of the garden. While she stood clear of the sparks, I'd burned Dad's things. Clothes, books, feathers, all the strange treasures he'd bring back to the house: seedpods and peculiar bits of bone; a bullet Old Pinnicke had dug from the body of a dead pig, the dull metal mushroomed into a flower; petrified wood. *There is no need to fill our minds with death and decay,* said my mother. She hated physicality, even sweat. *Is there, Bettina?*

Leaning out the door, Trish yelled, as if we were five, "Megarrity'll get you, Tina! Get in or get in the tray."

"There's a bird skull in the gatepost," I reported.

"Weirdos," said Trish.

I got in and we drove on. I couldn't see a house yet, just a track through an expanse of paddock, a few humped cattle that tossed their heads and trotted toward us, then away, switching their tails. A faint slope to a line of dark trees.

"Gwenda's a witch," said Trish casually.

"Self-styled," said Gary, as if there were gradations. "Herbs and cards."

"Sometimes she offers to help Dad solve crimes."

"Has it ever worked?" said Gary.

"What do you think? Look!" Trish pointed. A horse stood stock-still in the paddock. Not a horse. A sculpture. Bits of metal and timber. As we passed, it looked less horse-like, more skeletal, but also as if it was watching us.

"*That's* a crime," said Gary lightly. In spite of his tan, his freckles stood out.

"It's pretty good," said Trish. "Horrifying but, you know— art. The things you see from the corners of your eyes."

"Like the megarrity?"

"If we get stuck here in the dark, Gary Damson, I'll—"

They bickered. For no good reason, I was comforted. The truck swayed, lumbering into shadow as the track cut across a creek. Its bed was trampled mud, but here and there a patch of water, no larger than a hoof print, shone blue.

THE MEGARRITY

I don't know if anyone remembers where they first heard the tale of the megarrity. It's a story you tell camping, or on a veranda when no one switched a light on inside before the sun went down.

Gary's grandmother Vi, who had her own reasons, told it roughly this way, with variations depending on her listeners.

Once, on a bowl of dust beneath an iron sky, there lived a man whose name I won't tell you. This was before the great stations were cut up into farms, before there even were stations, back in the days when you could start a massacre and a war and finish both before the police arrived from a thousand miles away.

This man was tall and thin, tough as a side of old leather, but beneath the shade of his hat, his eyes were warm as a winter sky. I can't tell you whether he was a good man, but he cleared and felled and scratched a living of sorts from that ungentled earth, and he had brought such a wife with him! Black hair and amber eyes, sharp white teeth and gold freckles like fish-scales over her face and arms, and a fat baby held at her full breast. I can't tell you whether she was a good woman, but she knew the old ways of her own country, she worked hard and she did not question her husband when he said he was a plain, peaceful farmer, or complain when he returned from hunting with no meat, but blood (not his) on his boots and saddle blanket. So, as you see, he was more fortunate than most.

Around the rim of that little farm stood trees, and in those forests lived a clever-fingered, yellow-eyed, bronze-furred megarrity. Like many odd creatures, it had been carried idly away from its land, in a sea-chest perhaps, or on a shoulder or tangled like an albatross in rigging, or netted like a woman in rough clothes and bridal vows.

The megarrity did not know whether there was another like it anywhere in this country. It did not grieve—even far away among its own kind, it would have kept mostly to itself. For many years, all people knew of it was echoes among the trees. Megarrities, you know, are excellent mimics, while their attention holds. When this one tired of being itself, it would pass through the grass with the smoke-grey wallabies, frolic with possums along high branches, or lope like dusty dingoes between the trees.

But even a megarrity at times grows hungry and alone. The people who lived there among the hills took little notice of it, and the creatures which filled their stories had no time for a megarrity-come-lately, and turned their furred backs and their scaly tails. Besides, of late those folks had begun to avoid that stretch of country, or been driven away, or been killed by the farmer and his kind.

The megarrity took to wandering unseen into the herds of red cattle or among the dirty, shouldering sheep. It fed itself on calves and lambs, but it was tidy, and after it had gnawed them clean and sucked out the marrow, it always piled the white bones together and folded the skin neatly on top.

One day, the farmer took his gun into the trees, for he did not choose to share his calves and lambs. For a long time he rode; when the way grew too rough, he continued on foot, leading his horse.

The megarrity watched from the branches. When it could not help itself, it would echo the fall of the horse's hoof on a stone, or the snapping of twigs as the farmer pushed them aside. The farmer did not know enough to be suspicious. At last, however, his horse grew nervous. It tossed its head, rolled its eyes and refused to go further. Even so (for horses are sensitive, obstinate animals), the farmer might have disregarded this.

"Hey!" he shouted in surprise when the horse first shied.

"Hey!" called the megarrity. The farmer, trying to calm his mount, did not notice.

"Easy there, old fool," he said. "Whoa, gentle there."

("Old fool—gentle there," said the megarrity, enjoying itself.)

"Hush," whispered the farmer, rubbing the hollow above his horse's eye.

("Hush," whispered the megarrity as it leaned down close to hear him.)

Even in country like that, a whisper should not echo. The hairs on the farmer's back and arms and neck stood on end. But although he had been (until this tale) far too ignorant of megarrities, he was no stupider than most.

"Hullo?" he said.

"Hullo?" said the megarrity.

The farmer looked around. "Who's there?" he called.

"Who's there!"

"Come out and face me!" he said.

"Come out and face mc!" said the megarrity, hanging head-downward above the man, for all the world like the silver-green swags of leaves.

"You are a coward!" said the farmer.

"You are a coward!" agreed the megarrity (its voice was really very like his).

The horse had grown calmer, although it twitched its ears at every shout, and the farmer shook his head.

"I am a fool," he said, and the megarrity above him said enthusiastically, "You are a fool!"

The farmer took a great leap backwards and brought up his gun. There was the megarrity, clear as day, grinning at him upside-down with all its bright teeth and all its shining yellow eyes.

"Get out of my forest!" he said.

"My forest!" said the megarrity, swinging on its branch until the tree bent and swayed.

"I have a farm and a house, a wife and a fireside; I had cattle and sheep which you have eaten," said the farmer. "And I have a gun."

At that, he fired. He thought he must have hit the megarrity, for it dropped right down out of the trees.

It landed on his horse's back. The horse reared and bolted for home, the bridle trailing and the megarrity clinging to its back and throat and saddle with its bright, sharp claws.

The farmer had a long walk from there. The bush was empty of echoes, but at every sound, he jumped and looked around.

It was dark when he left the scrub and saw, across the moon-white bowl of the cleared paddocks, a friendly yellow light through the little windows and the long gaps in the walls of his slab hut.

He went to the window and, looking in, saw two sitting to dinner: his wife and himself. And himself looked up at the farmer in the window, and smiled with sharp, gleaming teeth.

"What shall I do?" thought the farmer. "I do not wish to frighten my wife, but I must get that creature with its long, bright claws out of there."

For whatever lies he told himself of being a man of peace, he knew at his heart, I think, that the megarrity loved cleverness and blood. It would settle comfortably into his own life, in his friendly slab hut with his golden bride and his whip and his guns.

The baby murmured in the room behind the curtain.

"It is the child," ventured the farmer outside the window.

"The child?" his wife echoed.

"It is the child," confirmed the megarrity, and watched the woman turn to the other room, where the infant twitched in its sleep.

"You are very clever," whispered the farmer through the gaps in the wall.

"I am very clever," said the megarrity.

"But it is a simple thing to be a farmer," whispered the man.

"A simple thing."

"I think you could not fool me that you are the jug of cream on the table."

"Fool you," giggled the megarrity, and turned into a jug of cream, just as blue, and hung about with the same fringe of beads. The farmer tried the door, but it was latched from within. The megarrity leaped off the table and prowled around, eye to eye with him through the gaps in the walls. The farmer could hear his wife singing an old, old lullaby.

He said, "Or that you are the fire."

Then the fire burned twice as hot, twice as fast in the hearth, and sparks roared up the chimney.

"Dear heart, the fire!" called his wife.

"I think you could not fool her that you are a snake," whispered the farmer.

"Fool her," agreed the megarrity. Next moment, the fire sank to ash. A snake, gleaming blue-black and beaded red, glided dust-dry from the hearth, with unblinking yellow eyes.

"Sso you see," it hissed, flickering its way along the packed-earth floor. "I am cleverer than you or her. I am the megarrity. Your people brought me here, but I ssshall be here after you vanissh into the treess."

Then the farmer's wife (who knew, after all, something of such things) brought the axe down hard, right behind the megarrity's head. She let the farmer in, and he slung the snake's body out on the rubbish pile and built a fire over it. Neither of them ever said anything more of it. If there was no sign of a snake's charred skeleton in the morning, why, any number of things might have carried it off in the night, leaving faint prints in the dust. And if often in the trees that farmer heard whispers, he always found he was speaking only to himself.

I remember—now, years ago—Mitch and Chris perched on the veranda railing, saying the megarrity ought to have eaten up the whole family.

"Then who'd have told the story?" Gary asked, lying back against the steps, his stiff red-brown hair almost touching my knee.

"The megarrity, idiot," said Chris. "Or the baby, if it lived. If *I* had been a megarrity, I'd have snuck in in the night and . . ."

Mitch grinned, face beaked and hungry in the shadows. "Left its bones in a tidy white pile and its skin folded neatly on top?"

"No, you'd have to hide it," Chris said. "Pretend to be it. I mean, you could get taken care of for the rest of your life."

"The rest of *their* lives, at least," said Mitch.

"Well," said Gary, loyal to his grandmother's telling of the story and to his family's trade, "I'd have taken bloody good care to keep it out to start with. Better locks and a really good fence."

I remember, too, Dad didn't like the story. "Make-believe," he said. "McGarrity's a good Scottish name. There's no beast called that."

That never stopped us echoing each other in the trees, though, just to get a rise.

CHAPTER FIVE

THE WITCH OF CARTER'S CROSSING

The truck bounced up from the creek's cool shadows and over a grid in a tidy fence—the only thing tidy about Gwenda Sage's place.

White tyre-swans spilled nasturtiums and geraniums; giant concrete toadstools squatted garish crimson in the mid-afternoon sun. *Tasteless.* Ornamental toads crouched, elbows out, leaching verdigris onto the cement rim of a pond green with weed and sharp with reflected dragonflies.

"This is nice," said Trish. I couldn't tell if she meant it.

The house sprawled at its ease, propped by pillows of banksia roses and yellow jasmine. The corrugated roof draped over the veranda like a cat in the sun.

Cats were everywhere, unconscious in the light, watchful in the shade. Coloured glass spun lazily in the windows. I should have been glad to be on solid ground again, but everything here made me itch, as if the place were pushing me away. The day's heat made the palms of my hands, the backs of my knees, the creases of my elbows sticky with sweat.

Gwenda Sage stood at the screen door, a wiry woman with a cloud of hair the colour of clay mud spilling down over her bare arms. A cat circled her ankles. She was thin and leathery, and her eyes were sharp. Whatever her relationship to the postmaster, she looked nothing like comfortable Mr Sage.

"Marilyn's boy?" She pointed secateurs at Gary. "*You* aren't meant to be here, Damson."

"Guess you want this," said Gary, holding up the mail. We picked our way across too-small stepping stones, through the garden.

Gwenda Sage gave a hefty sigh, pulled off gloves, rolled them around the secateurs and held out a dirty hand. Gary walked up the veranda steps, but Trish and I stayed in the sun.

"I smell smoke," I said. The scented smoke in my mother's room.

"Just incense," whispered Trish. "Cheap stuff."

"*You* can't come in," said Gwenda, looking at Gary as if over glasses, although she wasn't wearing any. "Who are those two?"

"Bettina Scott and Trish Aberdeen," said Gary flatly.

"Then they can't, either." She snorted. "Marilyn'll have your guts for garters. I've heard about *them*."

"I'm hoping you can help us," said Gary. "We're looking for someone from the back country. He goes by the name of

Smith. Light brown hair. Beard. Old Holden ute, cages on the back. There's another man with him, sometimes."

Gwenda Sage chuckled drily. "What do you have to do with that lot?" she replied to Gary. "Your mother really won't approve."

Her hands weren't dirty after all. My schoolyard scrapes had long faded (*Don't you think they're a bit fainter today, Bettina?*), but little black marks pitted Gwenda's hands and there were knotted white scars on her arms, which she hadn't covered up, although she was older than my mother.

"They've been here, once or twice," she said. "Wanted anything left in the sheds from when old Sylvie died."

"This was Sylvie Spicer's house?" said Trish, suddenly interested. "It doesn't look at all like the pictures on file—" She bit her lip. A police file? I wondered what had happened here.

Gwenda ignored her. "A few boxes of books, rotten. Some old crates and cages. Photos I guess your mum didn't want. Your dad would have told me to burn them, I bet." She gave Gary a yellow grin.

"My dad asked you to *stop* burning things," he said.

The woman shrugged. "Who's he to say what's garbage? Your mother inherited it, not him, and Marilyn sold it to me as-was, eventually. Any rate, the *Smiths* aren't welcome here anymore. Bit odd." She glanced at us speculatively. Trish crossed her arms.

"Aberdeen!" said Gwenda Sage abruptly, and jerked her chin at Trish. "*Your* dad never had time for me, neither."

"None of us are our dads," said Trish.

"Or our mothers," I ventured, startling myself. "Are we?"

"You'd be surprised," muttered Gwenda. "As for mothers . . ." She looked me up and down from my sandals to my hair, and sniffed.

"Miss Sage," prompted Gary.

"Gwenda Sage," said Trish, stepping forward. "*We've* got time for you. We're looking for someone who knows what happened to the Scott boys, and Mr Scott and Tina and my—" She paused, and gave a surprisingly helpless shrug. "Well, everything."

I hadn't considered that Trish might be looking for something too.

"What will you give me?" challenged Gwenda.

"I've given you your mail," said Gary.

"That's the law."

"I'll fix your gate," he said. I hadn't noticed anything wrong with it. "All right?"

Gwenda laughed. "Fence yourself out in future, then, along with the rest of them. You can come in, this once. You keep your word, though," she warned as Gary filed past. "You listen," (that to Trish), then to me, "And you hold your tongue and don't touch anything." She sniffed again, which was rude; even through the incense she smelled of sweat, dirt and burned metal. "Lemons," she said. The cat at her feet hissed.

Overstuffed sofas, piled with bright crocheted rugs and cushion-covers, crowded the sitting-room. Antique frames with domed glass had been filled with a collage of photos. Most were of a grinning schoolboy, but occasionally there was a younger Gwenda with startling hair and a garish dress. Dead flowers, stiff, gathered dust in dented brass vases, laced together by spiderwebs. Mother never liked cut flowers, not even everlastings.

There were packs of cards, too, but not playing cards, a thin book with the title in cursive, *We Meet in Dreams,* and several magazines of Spirituality and Ancient Wisdom, printed on thin paper.

I gingerly shifted these so I could sit. Headlines about cryptobotany, guardian grims, and the consciousness of stones slid grittily over each other. Gwenda Sage would probably get on with Old Pinnicke.

As she gave us lukewarm tea and damp shortbread creams, I ventured, "That was a handsome sculpture in the front paddock, Miss Sage." Politeness was always a safe option. "It is one of yours, isn't it?"

She didn't answer, just raised her sparse eyebrows and looked at Gary.

"Tina's brothers—Chris and Mitch Scott—took off," he said shortly.

"Boys will," said Gwenda.

"And Mr Scott, too," added Trish. "They found his car, smashed, but no sign of him."

"Like Uncle Davy—David Spicer," said Gary.

"And others," said Trish.

"Oh, I'd heard," said Gwenda. She sounded, of all things, satisfied.

"Meanwhile, Mrs Scott and Tina here—" Trish gestured at me, with habitual disgust. "Well, you didn't know her before. But the man—men—we're looking for might be able to explain what happened. It would help Tina. And Mrs Scott."

"Never met a helpful Scott," said Gwenda Sage. "Met a few who helped themselves."

"My father just *left*," I whispered, fiercely. It was important that he had chosen to go, although I couldn't say why. Strong emotions weren't attractive, but I clenched my hands until my short, presentable nails dug into my skin.

"Who ever really disappears?" said Gwenda Sage. "Things change, that's all. Damsons like everything neatly fenced in. Things change, but that's not the same as leaving."

"Miss Sage," began Gary.

"Hush," she said. "I'll tell you what I know, though it's precious little. But first, I have something to tell this Aberdeen girl. She can tell her father. He won't listen to me—not even my own brother ever listened to me—but he'll listen to her."

"He won't," said Trish.

Gwenda ignored her. "It's about what *really* happened in Woodwild."

"You've told him before," said Trish. "Dad's not superstitious. All we want to know—"

"Who said anything about superstition?" said Gwenda. "Pay attention."

Trish's nostrils narrowed; her eyes were wide.

"Manners," I whispered, hastily.

With a gusty sigh, Trish slid down among the patchwork cushions.

We were chasing the thinnest chance that the stranger who wrote *monsters* knew where my brothers were. If we refused to listen, Gwenda might not tell us where to find him.

The pull homewards to Runagate (where Sages were kindly and rational) was strong. I could give up, go back to my mother, be comfortable, stop trying to take my life into my own hands. I needn't see Trish, slouching inelegantly, or Gary, leaning forward with his blunt features intent, again. They would be happier without me.

I wanted to leave, very much. But it would be rude. I sat quietly, hands folded in my lap.

THE SCHOOL IN THE WILDERNESS

Nothing is as it was (said Gwenda). Once, when you were too small to care, when I was Gwenda Alleman, there was still a town called Woodwild. It made the third point of the triangle of Runagate and Carter's Crossing. Woodwild was larger than Runagate, and looked down on it, in elevation as well as spirit: it still had two pubs, a grid of comfortable streets under leaning ironbarks, a grocery store and—outside of town on a side track, in its own paddock—a school. OUR CHILDREN ARE OUR FUTURE, said the sign outside.

It used to be that the verges of the Runagate-Woodwild

Road were lined with flowering lantern-bush, studding the scrub with clutches of coloured stars: white, golden, crimson and violet. Handsome, if you didn't think about it too hard. It came to this country as a garden shrub. Once it got here, it grew faster than any plant had a right to. Strange, what chooses to flourish here. Which plants. Which stories.

Those glorious vines strangled trees and bushes and blocked creeks. They poisoned animals, and crept under houses to force the floorboards off their beams. Old Pinnicke would put on an ancient dinner jacket and a German helmet to fight through them, when he went out in the evening to bring his milking cow home.

It grew faster than it could be cut; it burned slower than everything around it. People tried dragging it down with chains, digging it up, burying it, poisoning it. Scientists asked for grants; politicians offered rewards to anyone who could kill the stuff.

By the time Terrence—my husband, then—and I saw our Jim in seventh grade, lantern-bush was strangling Woodwild.

The mayor—also president of the Woodwild Progress Association—announced at a town meeting, by flyers printed in pungent purple ink on the school's mimeograph, by word of mouth and an advertisement in the *STAR,* that anyone who could rid Woodwild and its surrounds of the pest would be given five hundred dollars, the region's gratitude, and a memorial hall.

Subscriptions raised the reward to a thousand dollars, but no one claimed it. Woodwild resigned itself to its fate. Graziers started to leave for country where lantern-bush hadn't taken root or wasn't so virulent. Businesses starved.

Woodwild gave up on science altogether. And that winter, *he* arrived.

He drove up the Runagate-Woodwild Road in his station wagon—not a car for rattling over corrugations—throwing dust over the tangled hedges of lantern-bush, which was in flower. It was always in flower.

Vines were climbing over the sign that said:

WELCOME TO WOODWILD.
HEART OF THE BUSH.
"A FRIENDLY TOWN"

He drove past it, straight up to the gate in front of the veranda where old Hilda Damson sat with her dogs, half-asleep. Where the rest of the Damsons were, I don't know—never where they're wanted. Then without asking directions, or permission, or even nodding, he turned, took the right track and pulled into Woodwild.

He had pale hair. He himself was so pale he almost glowed, as if he spent all his time inside. That way all over, I promise you. Beautiful. Well, I wasn't so bad myself, although you should have seen my hair! His name was Darryl. That was all I knew.

He put up at the Stockman's Arms and soon the whole town had heard: he was from the coast, had a set of bagpipes, meant to win that reward. I won't pretend I wasn't one of the gossips—Terrence wasn't interested, so I had to tell someone.

Some people said he brought an animal with him, but they couldn't agree what type. Peg Hale, who held the licence, said she never saw it. She'd have turned it out—him, too. But I cleaned his room, and all the times I was there *I* never noticed anything.

Pinnicke—Billy Pinnicke, Old Pinnicke's father—who had an enormous white beard and played the accordion at dances, shook his head. "Never trust a piper," he told me. But when he saw the pipes, he changed his tune. "No bagpipes I've ever seen," he grumbled, as he sat in the bar day after day. "Too many legs."

Old Pinnicke muttered too, but he always did. Our visitor was the only man I ever knew take notice of the Pinnickes' stories. And he laughed, asked for a map, and spread it on the bar.

Men went up, looked over Darryl's shoulder and started to point out landmarks: this gully is where the bushranger had his last stand, that's the sinkhole where at midday you hear a horse but don't see one, there's the stock route along the edge of the old Spicer station—*not* haunted, of course, but no one likes to go there at night—and that's as far as Woodwild will admit an interest; if you live beyond there, you belong to Runagate. There's the old sawmill and the new. They marked the worst stands of lantern-bush, always on their own properties.

Not that they liked the man or believed he'd work a miracle. But if there *was* something in it, they didn't want to lose out.

Then, sitting in the bar of the Stockman's Arms, Darryl put those pipes together. The men—in Woodwild, never ahead of the times, most women didn't care to be seen in the main bar, though it had been legal for years—watched as he twisted wooden tubes into leather bags, tightened joints with waxed cord and plumber's tape, and tuned them with rounds of sticky paper over the holes. Careful, as if he knew what he was doing (or wanted us to think so) but hadn't done it a lot. You know what I mean.

Terrence, of course, thought himself above being interested.

Once Darryl pumped up those pipes and let them go, they made an unholy noise (Billy Pinnicke said). There did seem to be more sticks and valves and bellows than strictly necessary. But they were bagpipes, after all. Since the Pinnickes played accordions, it was the pot calling the kettle.

When Darryl left the bar, the kids sitting on their school ports eating ice creams in the warm winter sunshine jumped up and ran after him, shouting. They threw pebbles at the pipes, but he laughed, and the crows flew along shouting just as loud.

I didn't think much in those days, or I might have yelled those kids to heel. Sent them home. Not that it would have helped in the end.

He kept walking after his followers tired, and where he walked, he played. You could hear him from anywhere in town. From the Stockman's Arms, from the school itself, even in Hale Motors over the rumble of engines and drills. My Jim said if he were a plant, that sound'd make him curl up and die.

For a whole week, Darryl walked around Woodwild, going out a mile or so at dawn when dew silvered the grass, working through bush and paddocks, coming in dirt-reddened at evening, his fine skin sun-singed. The grocer said the drone of the pipes set his teeth on edge. The mayor's cockatoo lost its feathers and had to be moved into the pub's kitchen to keep warm.

Hilda Damson never said a word—she was all for letting nature take its course, as I remember, yet I don't recall any lantern-bush ever troubling that house.

Darryl made slow progress: it's hard going in lantern-bush scrub, even with all your breath about you. People jeered, but he'd laugh back, showing his teeth. He didn't act crazy—apart from the bagpipes.

He'd bring things back he'd found. A bit of iron, a glass bottle-stop, a wallaby skull white in his hand. I made him keep them in his car, not the room—Peg Hale wouldn't have approved, and they gave me the horrors.

The next fortnight, he drove further. He played his pipes in paddocks and gullies, on rocky outcroppings and the verge of the Runagate-Woodwild Road. Cats cleared out and weren't seen for a month. Pelicans flew off course and landed in the Pinnickes' dam, and all the magpies began attacking, though it wasn't nesting season.

In the end, there can't have been a patch of lantern-bush near Woodwild that hadn't heard those pipes. He even paid my Jim to show him the chalk-caves, and played there, with that animal of his—clambering over the boulders as if born to it, for all his canvas shoes and city skin. I asked what the animal was, for I swear I never got a look at it. Jim shrugged and said it had been dark.

I'd wake at midnight, thinking I heard the echoes of the piping chasing around down there, under the rocks and roots. Sometimes I still do.

Then he left. He said he'd be back at the end of summer.

"Good riddance," said my husband. "He's too smooth by half. All a scam, you'll see. We'll move to the coast, find work, send Jim to a good school."

"Darryl was telling me about the sea," I said. I'd never seen it. Still haven't.

"Or maybe we'll move further inland," Terrence said. Terrence Alleman wasn't a violent man. If he'd picked a fight early on, it might have made Darryl a mite less comfortable. Might have changed any number of things.

Life went on, a little quieter. Work and dances, gossip and church. Weddings. Funerals. The lantern-bush, always flowering, was unusually brilliant that spring. You could smell it on the sunlight.

But as the weather got hotter, the vines curled back on themselves where they'd usually have stretched out, grasping. They shrivelled in the summer sun, leaves withering black.

Then the news said the government was bringing in a beetle from wherever lantern-bush had come from, to lay its eggs in the roots. It would kill them forever, across the whole state. The beetles probably wouldn't kill anything else. They had been cleared to be released, they had been released, the lantern-bush was dying everywhere.

By then, farmers were worrying about drought and fire and flood. We'd almost forgotten the vines when the mayor unveiled the statue bought with the thousand dollars: a beetle triumphant on a bronze bouquet of lantern-bush.

"Science," he declared, "has given our children a future!" Science, of course, was expected not to care about thousand-dollar rewards.

The next day, Darryl returned to Woodwild.

This time he put up at the Jubilee Hotel, a rickety wooden place opposite the Stockman's: him, his pipes and (perhaps) his animal. Peg Hale was shirty with me, as if it were my fault he didn't take a room from her, as if we'd fought. But Darryl and I hadn't parted on bad terms. We hadn't parted on any terms at all.

He arrived in the evening. I heard he went straight to his room—alone, as far as I know. He spent the next morning driving, looking around, watched suspiciously by my husband and by everyone else who'd heard him play the winter before. Then he parked at the Jubilee and walked to stand with his hat pushed back, considering the statue. I got a look then: sun and dirt had taken more of a hold on him—there were lines at his eyes and scars on his knuckles I didn't remember. And a ring, the bastard. If I'd known . . . well, life would run a lot differently if anyone knew the half of what would turn out to have been useful. His smile, though, *glittered* more; he moved as if he'd grown up—knew more about the world.

Then he went to the mayor's house, and anyone who knows anything can guess what was said.

Afterwards, he slung the bag of pipes over his shoulder and stepped down off the veranda of the Jubilee Hotel, taking his animal with him. Although it might have been a stray cat, or a shadow. Billy Pinnicke said it was a creature like that instrument, with too many legs—but he was very old.

Darryl started up playing with a groan away near the school, round and round it. If anyone in town hadn't known he was back, they learned it then.

Then he walked back to the hotel, got his duffle bag, bundled it and the pipes into the back seat of his car, climbed into the front and drove away.

"I'm going to see what that teacher has to say," said Peg Hale to me. "You mind the bar, you like men so much."

But the next man to come in was Terrence. He opened his mouth, saw me, shut it again. He was going to blame me for Darryl. Just because I'd been *friendly* with the man a year before.

"Those plants put up a fight?" laughed Billy Pinnicke.

But Terrence looked, blank, at me. "The school's gone," he said.

I didn't believe him. Even when I saw.

Except for the glint of sunlight on the topmost edge of its high water tank, nothing of the school could be seen but lantern-bush newly sprung: a dense scrub of writhing vines, malevolent with flowers. It spilled onto the road, even covered the little horse paddock where one or two students still left their ponies.

When Terrence stopped the car, I swear I saw a branch lengthening, putting out leaves, spikes and flowers, stretching until it reached a faint track in the grass and stopped, as if it had grown there for years.

"Reckon that's where your man walked round," said Old Pinnicke, pointing with a stick to the bent grass and the dry dust under it, marked with the soles of tennis shoes. "Round and round, and up jump the weeds."

Billy Pinnicke shook his head. "Can't trust pipers," he said.

"Where's Jim?" Terrence asked me.

"In school, of course!" I snapped. He was the reporter; he was meant to know these things. My stomach knotted. "Where else should he be?"

"World's full of people not where they should be," said Old Pinnicke.

I started to run along the edge of the hedge. When had I last been here? Time enough for a few plants to spring up, surely. I tried to convince myself Terrence was trying to frighten me, in revenge for—well, we were barely together anymore by then. I tried to walk, to breathe.

The school bus, familiar rust blooming through its blue and white paint, was trapped half-out of the bushes, flowers nodding through a shattered window. The driver stood beside it, pale. "Just came up, didn't it," he kept saying.

I suppose I wasn't the only one asking questions, looking for a way in, but all I recollect is my hands feeling as if I'd plunged them into ice, and my lungs on fire. "Maybe Jim went with him, to show him the caves," I remember saying to Terrence when he caught up with me, although I'd seen Darryl drive away.

I remember, too, seeing the body of a topknot pigeon bobbing on a high spray, pierced by a thorn.

The hedge didn't grow any further. The man who kept the hardware store leant a ladder against the bushes and, carefully, climbed up. He was almost to the top when the rungs slowly sank into the vines; he had to scramble and slide down to the ground again. When Bob Hale put on thick leather welding gloves and pushed his hand into the leaves, the spikes bit into it and he could only get his arm free by leaving the glove behind. Even then, he had long bloodied gouges down his arm.

The mayor sent for hedge-clippers, and graziers brought horn tippers and bolt cutters and hacked into the branches. But when we reached past broken stems, new spikes struck up, and the vines never seemed weaker or thinner. The scratches festered for days. The scars up my arms are from thorns, whatever Terrence says.

Old Pinnicke even produced a rusted cavalry sword.

"What's that meant to do?" sneered Terrence. When he was afraid, he was always unkind and entirely *reasonable*. No one wanted to say it simply seemed *right* when faced with impossible hedges. "Is this a fairy tale? When he gets in, who's he going to kiss to wake them—the teacher?"

That was another thing no one wanted to mention: before this, we had never heard the school below a dull roar on a weekday. Now only branches hissed and grated.

"There's an explanation," said Terrence. I had to remind myself our Jim was there, and Terrence must be feeling it. "They'll call in Primary Industries and Pest Control."

"It grew in a day," said Peg Hale. "Science doesn't do that, Terrence."

"Besides," wheezed Billy Pinnicke, though I wouldn't like to say he was laughing. "If it's a story, it's not that sleeping one. That one was about not getting invited. And you did invite that piper, Mr Mayor. We all did."

"Some more than others," said Terrence darkly.

A policeman arrived from Runagate, for all the good *that's* ever done. An ambulance and a real fire engine came from further away. But there wasn't anything for them to put out, or anyone to put in the ambulance. Tractors and dozers roared slowly up the road, though even ordinary lantern-bush hedges never yielded easily to them.

It was too green to burn. But someone doused the vines with petrol and *that* caught alight. Evening had fallen. Red flames and black smoke billowed up, and a woman screamed. They probably say it was me. I still wake up and think I've heard it—but this was all a long time ago. Even grief gets tired.

It kept the firies busy for a while. "It was an idea," said Terrence, wandering back. "Nobody else was doing anything."

Someone was sobbing, "They'll kill them, they'll kill them." But no one talked more about burning.

Even a rescue helicopter came—the first we'd seen. It had a searchlight. The vines tangled and thrashed in the downrush of air. The flowers shone ghastly white in its beam. Later, I heard the pilot said the hedge must have been there for years. It covered the whole paddock, with only an old water tank, spindly-legged on its timber stand, sticking above it. Fire trap, he said. That would be the story. Even the newspaper couldn't think of another way to run it, although Terrence had been right there and saw it clear as I did.

Next day, the singed bushes were already greening up. The

grocer seized a shovel and ran at them. He howled, beating the branches; most of us joined him. I still think if the bloody aloof Damsons had deigned to help instead of letting things *take their course* . . .

For a minute, that hedge shrank back. Then it reared up and crashed down, coiling and thrashing. Most of us got clear, although some were badly cut and whipped about. Terrence dragged me away, telling me not to make an exhibition of myself—he had the nerve, later, to tell me I didn't seem to *care*.

But the grocer had beaten his way in further than the others and didn't even try to get free. Next, he was a metre deep behind leaves and spines and flowers. He didn't scream, even though his feet left the ground—he just fought forward until he disappeared. Only a little blood on a few yellow flowers remained.

After that, even the birds kept away.

It was a fire, they said. They kept saying it, even while lantern-flowers bloomed bright as flame. I suppose there are things police aren't trained to deal with. Though there are others, if they'd cared to get involved.

A fire. If you say things often enough, people believe it. Even parents calling the names of their children near the school. Even the grocer's wife leaving plates of food among the bunches of garden flowers, the lonely dew-drenched toys. The next morning, the plates were broken and empty.

I sat there with her one night, though Terrence said I was a fool. "We all were!" I'd told him. I'd forgotten how cold night was, outside, as if the heat just dropped out of the day and you could touch the stars.

We heard the vines. Not the uneven whisper of the wind, but something moving through them. Carefully. Quickly.

We waited. Then Amelia—the grocer's wife—turned on the torch.

For a heartbeat the light showed massed pale leaves, glittering thorns and between them a darkness with two shining yellow eyes. A long, blackened arm, skeletal, stretched a clawed, clutching hand to the dish. Then it *hissed* at us.

I ran, towing Amelia. She had to be sent away after that. The store closed.

"It was a feral cat," said Terrence.

Billy Pinnicke said, "It was that piper's animal. It'd be getting hungry, nothing left but bugs and casserole. No one saw it with him when he left." But no one was certain they'd seen it when he arrived, either.

The world forgot we'd ever had a school. In Woodwild, it felt as if the vines had grown inside our skulls. We'd never get past them. No kiss could fix *that*.

The few students who'd been sick, or smoking up in the creek, were sent to boarding school. Their parents didn't stick around long. The grocery store was already closed. The mayor looked like he'd aged twenty years.

The town was failing when Old Pinnicke drove in with the grocer's gold chain in his pocket. He'd been checking traps deep in the scrub, and one of his dogs had found it. Everyone knew that chain, swinging off the grocer's hairy chest while he bent over, wrapping cold groceries in newspaper to keep on long drives.

The police *investigated*. They went into steep country and gullies. They found dying stands of lantern-bush, sheep bones, cattle bones, rusting carcasses of cars. They went right into the caves. I heard a rumour they found a cavern nearly beneath the school, the stone white in light filtering down through knotted roots. Nothing else.

I don't know if they looked for Darryl. He never showed his face in Woodwild again, but I reckon he didn't go far. He'd taken his chance to spy out the land; more than once I saw him drive by me on the roads. The nerve of the man. But no one wanted to know. I suppose if once they started questioning the piper, there were too many other things they'd need to start believing. Other people they'd need to start blaming.

Woodwild curled up and died. A few people moved to Carter's Crossing or Runagate—a thing like that can pin you to a place, whether you want to stick around or not. Maybe Billy Pinnicke's still in the dark bar of the Stockman's Arms. Peg Hale left to live with one of her daughters. She had a lot. The mayor took to drink, left his cockatoo behind and went away.

As the town emptied, the trees clustered around it, the quiet ringing with cricket-voices and the silence of the Woodwild school bell. And in the heart of Woodwild, I daresay, that beetle stands triumphant on its bronze plinth, in the only place in the country where lantern-bush still grows wild.

Sometimes, people still find bones in the scrub. Here and there. Mostly you wouldn't think to ask if they were human. They're weathered and old, and some of them are small, and marked by thousands of tiny scratches, as might be left by age. Or teeth.

CHAPTER SIX

THE OLD FARM

"It was a fire," Gary said at last, as we drove out of Gwenda Sage's scornful grief into the strong white light of late afternoon. "Everyone knows that. If it had been a—a *piper,* Mr Scott of all people . . . That's who she meant, isn't it?"

"Who are you trying to convince?" said Trish, absently irritable, as if the story hadn't been the one she'd wanted to hear. "It's hardly the only disappearance he's linked with."

"Not as a suspect," replied Gary.

"What does your grandmother say happened?" said Trish.

"We Damsons keep up fences, walk boundaries," said Gary. "We don't get involved." His face was twisted. I didn't think he believed his own words. "Lantern-bush is just a weed. Besides, even if . . . how do you undo *that*?"

I wanted to say, "It will be all right." But Trish glared sideways at me. I doubted my careful words would be welcomed. And his family had never liked mine.

As for my family—Gwenda Sage hadn't talked to the men we were looking for since she first bought the land from Gary's mum, when she'd sold them the rubbish Sylvie Spicer left behind. She hadn't liked them, and they knew they weren't welcome, she said (I thought unbidden of the bird skull in the gate), but she'd seen them drive past now and then. She said to look for them up the back roads, toward Woodwild.

I tried to picture the abandoned town; no image formed. *An imagination is a frivolous thing to cultivate, isn't it, Bettina,* so instead, I'd read books about keeping poultry, and efficient homemaking, and manners.

Darryl, Gwenda had called the piper. Of course no one believed her. I imagined my dad, young and pale-haired, with a smile cruel as the new moon. But he had been proud of me, once.

"Urban exploration," pronounced Trish, thoughtfully. She took out a cigarette, but Gary told her off. "A whole ghost town. Why didn't we ever go up there?"

"There's not much to see," said Gary, "It's—" He shut his mouth.

"You've *been* there?" Trish sat up straight. "When?"

"With my dad once. Boundary works. And my gran still lives in the old Damson house. It's just—" He shrugged. "I don't like ruins."

"I do," said Trish, with relish. "There should be more of them."

I opened the gate. When he'd driven through, Gary got out too, leaving Trish to brood with her feet on the dashboard. He took the bird skull from the hollow post, delicately, muttering, "Knew they weren't welcome . . . I bet ghosts would be," and spent some time tightening wires, with an arrangement of ratchets and levers and clawed chains. He scuffed the dirt clear of grass and bark and frail things: beetle shells or bird bones. Then he fetched a box from one of the tin trunks on the back of the truck and scattered powder around the base of the posts, along the fence line a little way in each direction. Salt, perhaps, or poison against white ants.

I watched closely, propriety straining against curiosity.

"It's a start, anyway," said Gary. He washed his hands with the jerry can of water in the back and dried them on his shirt. "Keeping the fences clear, *marking* them, is the main thing, really." But he didn't sound sure. "I'll come back and fix it up better." He glanced at me. I knew Trish was watching us in the mirror, she sat so still.

"What happened to your arm?" He took it and turned it, wrist upwards. I'd been right; I did know the feeling of Gary Damson's hands. Not angry, but forthright. There were the scratches left by Gwenda's fingers: the curl of white-grazed skin, a few beads of blood.

"It's just a scrape," I said. "It will heal soon."

"Gwenda did that?"

"She held me back, when we were leaving." Gwenda Sage hadn't said anything, only looked hard as if trying to see my dad in me, but her nails had dug into my arm, like she'd hoped to feel something other than flesh and bone under my skin. "It was an accident." Accidents don't need to be explained, or forgiven.

"I've got disinfectant in the—"

"Look," I said. "It's barely there." I brushed away the dry skin. "The bruises you're making will last longer."

He wasn't holding my wrist tight, but he let go quickly. I felt a moment's triumph and straightened my cardigan with meaningful primness.

"Do we keep going, Tina?" he asked.

"Bettina," I said, mostly from habit. *Home.* To Runagate, easy in the sunlight. To the garden, the chooks talking softly among themselves. Our white fence. No stories of lost towns or echoing caverns. No inconvenient memories. I smelled lemon flowers, blowing like lace curtains; frail as lace, pierced by the strong light. My mother would be awake soon.

Bloody aloof Damsons, Gwenda had said. Gary hadn't talked to me for three years, but he was now. *Your mother really wouldn't approve.*

I wasn't the only person straining against what they had taught themselves to believe. "Yes," I said, before I could let myself think better of it.

Gary looked worried and relieved at the same time.

"Oh, *come on,*" said Trish, when he didn't turn back the way we'd come. "What are we going to do? Hope we pass someone who's seen two men who probably don't even exist? You're just driving for the hell of it. I wanted to ask my dad—" She bit her lip. "I'll miss dinner."

"You heard Gwenda," said Gary.

"We all did," said Trish. "Gwenda cheated on Terrence Alleman, which is understandable, the school burned down, she blames herself and the Damsons—I'm coming around to her way of thinking on that—and she's not all there. It's hot. I'm hungry. I want to go home."

"Tina doesn't," said Gary.

Trish swore, but this time, she didn't turn her nose up at the wilted sandwiches.

We ate in silence and drove along back roads, jolting over corrugations, through rocky creek beds and over cattle grids, each lost in our own thoughts, losing ourselves in the trees. Once we saw a sign. "Look," said Trish. Gary slowed. Its faded paint was peeling. A carcase had hung from it: a few shreds of dry hide remained, and vertebrae strung like beads.

"Pinnicke's work," said Gary grimly. "Dingo. Probably."

"Someone has to do it, don't they?" I asked, but no one answered. *Yes, they do,* I told myself. My mother rarely asked rhetorical questions. I looked away from the twisted corpse to the words on the sign. "Old Woodwild Road," I read aloud. Beneath the sign, like stars, bobbed a single stem of lantern-bush.

"Ugh," said Trish. Gary drove on.

The road curved across a ghost of its own drifting dust. Ahead was the rough, unsealed surface, striped gold and violet with tree shadows. The rough bark of the overarching limbs was black as blood, and the deepening yellow sun shone through the leaves like a lantern. Sudden as waking, I recognised this place.

"Here!" I said, and drummed my hands lightly on the dashboard, startling Gary. "Turn here, we're nearly there."

"Where?" said Trish as Gary steered us through a gap in the trees. There was no sign; the narrow way was poorly graded.

"I've never been down here," he said.

I didn't know either. Yet here was another turning into a track soft with sand, and ahead there would be a slope of tumbled red-stained stone; the road would swerve around it, back into line with the lazy loops of fence wire. And so it did.

Bettina likes to stay in sight of Runagate, don't you dearest? I only remembered living in town. But I had been here before, and I felt light in my veins.

"What about the men with the geese?" said Trish. "Are we just sightseeing now?"

"If Tina knows this place—" began Gary.

"*If*," said Trish.

"—maybe the boys did too. It can't be coincidence."

"It can," said Trish.

When we reached the rusted white gate at the end, I opened the door and dropped to stand on the earth. Dirt sifted between the straps of my sandals. Bird feet had made pale patterns across older prints of tyres. A rusted chain, padlocked, held the gate shut, but the key was kept under a stone at the base of the fencepost. The certainty poured through me like sunshine. I found it at once.

"A key," said Gary flatly, while I rubbed the rust off my hand.

"You've been holding out on us," said Trish.

But I shook my head. I was only remembering this as we found it, the further we drew from Runagate: along the track rutted and hollowed with braided gullies left by rain, meandering between slim saplings, their squared leaves lit gold. Each turn felt like the beat of my own heart.

Halfway along, Gary stopped. He made us get out so he could pull the seats forward and unlock a long, thin box, from which he took a shotgun, darkly gleaming and beautiful as a snake.

"Just in case," he said, and looked from one of us to the other.

"Give it to me," said Trish, and took it with a grimace, although her hands were sure. "Tina isn't exactly going to be much help."

"We're helping Tina," Gary reminded her, and glanced uncertainly at the scrub, the hills, the sagging fence wires. His breezy confidence had faded. He closed his door quickly, and before we drove on, I heard the echo rolling around the emptiness of the trees.

Howling wilderness, my mother had once called the bush beyond town. Dad had laughed.

My heart sat high in my chest. I was more alive and more scared than I had been for years. Ahead of us, through the gilded saplings and the dense old scrub, we would find it: a house, half-staggering beneath a weight of banksia roses, and a shed, and marvels.

"We aren't necessarily going to find . . . them," said Trish. "Mitch and Chris, I mean. It's been three years since they took off." *Monsters.* "They won't still be in Inglewell. Anyone could live here. What if it's those men you saw? I mean, if *Gwenda Sage* thinks people are odd, I don't want to meet them."

It could be my dad, I thought, rustily—I'd so carefully *not* thought that. *If all those stories mean anything, they mean sometimes people do just disappear. And maybe they can be found.*

"If it even is them," continued Trish. "They could have changed." Gary patted her knee, and she jumped. "People do," she added, fiercely.

We drove out of the saplings, over a grid woven through by green blades and into a house paddock tumbled with unkempt plants—I recognised the pale yellow of rosella flowers among the green panic grass, the vast abrasive hearts of pumpkin leaves between castor-oil shrubs. Gary stopped and cut the engine. Trish passed the plastic canteen—the water tasted stale—and we looked at the house.

It slanted, grey, vacant windows gaping. Where I wanted there to be banksia roses, there was a clawing skeleton of bare branches. At the top of the open flight of steps, a screen door banged in the breeze. One of the lower steps was missing and had been replaced by a drum. There was a smell of oil and of dogs, and the low afternoon murmuring of birds and, beyond, the distant thump of a generator.

"Hello?" called Gary, but no one answered. He jumped down and went up the steps. I followed at his heels. Trish stayed at the truck. Just in case, she said.

Gary caught the screen door as it swung open on the wind.

"No!" I said, anxious for him. Everything I knew was stretched over a dark pit, and I didn't want Gary to disappear into it, too. "You don't really want to go in, do you, Gary?"

He frowned back. "Don't pull that on me, Tina. I'll make my own mind up. All right? I don't know if I'm talking to you or your mum, half the time. If you don't want me to go in, tell me why, and let me decide."

"All right," I said, startled. Gary shrugged as if brushing something off and went inside.

A little hot anger pooled at the base of my throat. I wanted to make him listen to me, for his own good. *Please* tasted bitter.

I said nothing, and followed him into the kitchen.

Ropes of soot-blackened cobwebs hung from the ceiling. The floor was layered with rotting newspaper. Green scum sat in the sink, and unwashed dishes were piled in it and across the table. Cans of food—full and empty and open but half-finished—were stacked by the wall.

I stopped while Gary walked ahead, the light through dirty windows dulling his hair.

It wasn't decent. This room had once been clean and bright—I could picture lace blowing at the windows and linoleum shining. Horror, and all my mother's training, swallowed my annoyance at Gary Damson. People shouldn't live like this. Even monsters.

"What are you doing?" he demanded, returning silently a minute later.

I nearly jumped out of my skin. Gary reached past me and turned off the stream of dirty water I had choked from the faucet.

"There's no hot water," I said helplessly.

Gary studied me and sighed. "Put down the soap and come on."

The spark of resentment rekindled. I set the gritty grey bar down firmly. "So, you can tell *me* what to do—"

"I don't remember ever being able to make you listen," said Gary. As we went down the unsteady stairs, he asked, "Do you often barge into people's houses and do their dishes?"

"But if it's Chris and Mitch . . ." I hesitated, not wanting to say *and Dad*. He wouldn't live like that.

"Anything?" interrupted Trish from the truck, glancing away from the high, leafy circle of the horizon. "Food?"

"Filth and a room of books eaten by mice," said Gary. "Looked like confetti. There's no one home. We'll try down the back."

"We're going to get shot at for trespassing. Or by accident," said Trish, looking at the shotgun in distaste. "I'm putting this away. We should call my dad."

"I didn't see a phone," said Gary. "Keep it handy."

He rolled the truck down between the trees behind the

house. The undergrowth was thick on either side, a wilderness of shrubs and straw-dry grass, barbed wire and curling tin—the bones of machines unmade. That grieved me a little.

Beyond stood the shed: a structure of timber and galvanised iron. The end facing us was in blue shadow, but along the side, sunlight glanced dull fire off opaque windows. The high sliding doors on the near wall were closed and padlocked; although the planks were warped, we couldn't see anything between them. "It's insulated," said Gary.

"There's a door on the other end," I said, without thinking.

Gary drove around, and there it was. Just as I remembered. We climbed out.

The door had a latch of folded metal, but it was unfastened, its broken lock sunk in the dirt near the toe of my sandal. Gary pushed at the lock with his boot.

"They didn't need to break in. The key was under the tyre," I said, puzzled.

"Tina," hissed Trish, glancing uncomfortably at the screen of saplings. "Whose place is this?"

Mine seemed the wrong answer, but I heaved aside a rotting tyre that leaned against the wall, trammelled by grass. There, pressed into the ground like a fossil, almost the same colour as the dirt, was the key. "I don't know," I said, although the ground beating up through my thin soles said *home, home,* as surely as the garden in Upper Spicer Street ever did.

"But you've been here before, right?" Trish asked. It was odd to know—or suspect—more about my life than she did.

"I'm guessing it's where the Scotts lived before they moved to Runagate," said Gary.

Trish pulled a face and put her ear to the door. She'd put the shotgun back in its trunk, but since we were going inside, Gary didn't protest. All we heard was the thump of the generator.

"What's in there?" she demanded.

Wonders. "I don't know," I said.

"H-Hello!" shouted Gary, and knocked, his first blow uncertain. I tried to be anxious, but the earth and the grass and the evening breeze surrounded me, as if I had been set into a socket of the world for which I'd been designed.

Still no answer.

Inside, the shed smelled of mice and dry decay. A naked lightbulb hung from the ceiling, casting stark shadows on benches and tools, entangled cords and the gutted corpses of machinery. There were open, swollen boxes of paper, mouse-eaten, and on the floor downy feathers turned and shuffled in a draught. Metal frameworks, complicated by the shadows, were propped against the wall. Bones. Structures of wings nailed to boards.

"Don't tidy up," said Gary. I wrapped my arms around myself and kept my hands under my elbows.

An underlying intent showed through the mess. Years of failings piled on each other. Trish rifled through documents on the nearest bench, pushed back the lid of a box. The paper inside was almost chewed through; flat, swivelling insects scurried from between the sheets. I stepped away quickly.

"This doesn't make any sense," she said. "It looks like calculations, but . . ." She held up the paper. "I don't recognise half of these words. And the handwriting's terrible. This isn't even English."

Mould-mottled envelopes, their stamps dull. Magyarország, Ísland, Åland. But these had been addressed to Darryl Scott, not Nerida, and the handwriting was vigorous, angular and crabbed. They did not smell of flowers.

"Don't— Just, be careful," said Gary, stalking catlike between the benches. He'd picked up one piece of paper, then put it down, rubbing his hands on the sides of his jeans.

Trish looked askance at both of us, and moved on. "Weird," she said. "There's bagpipes here."

Gwenda's story. Dad in Woodwild, but not here.

"Probably full of moths," said Trish.

A spidery leg brushed my arm and I leaped sideways, striking a shelf. No. Not a spider. A withered twig, its leaves long fallen. Other branches had been nailed to the walls. I breathed again.

My mother's voice, faint in my ear, told me I'd never been here, and yet—I touched the shelves without looking, felt beneath the silk of dust a split stick. A dowsing rod, I knew.

Here was a curved stone: fossil wood picked out in opal. Cicada shells, their amber husks rustling in a cigar box. I remembered my father plucking one from a branch, hollow as a memory of sunlight.

"*On the Track of Unknown Animals.*" Trish had found a set of books and was reading their titles portentously. Gary did not laugh, and twitched when Trish dropped them back on the shelf.

Another stone, this one an axe head Dad had found, he said, in the paddock. A fogged jar holding brittle relics of statice, rice-flower, everlasting daisies, delicate as my mother. The faded paper blossoms of lantern-bush. Another jar of fine bones.

All this is how you can make the world work for you. I could almost hear Dad's voice in the stale air of the shed. He hadn't let the boys play in here. They had been monsters, after all.

One day, I'll explain. But he had gone away, and my mother had told me not to worry, I was hers. And I had forgotten.

Something banged against the far end of the shed. I jumped, my heart in my mouth. Trish swore indelicately. Gary stood still, pale as he'd been when he almost hit me with his truck.

The thumping was repeated, resounding off the iron roof. Trish and Gary both walked toward it. I looked behind us at the open door, then followed. Gary picked a hammer up off a bench as he passed—he held it more easily than he had the shotgun.

Something scraped the other side of the wall, and a voice whined through it, "I know you're there, nibbling like a mouse. Won't you set me free, poor thing?"

"Who's there?" demanded Gary.

The voice was silent for a moment then, sounding put out, said, "You aren't my sister. Where is T-T-Tina?"

"What do you want with her?" said Trish.

"What will she want with me?" asked the voice—muffled, but sounding near tears. "Nobody wants a wicked monster. A wicked wild monster, poor thing, poor boys, nobody to s-save them. Only knives and the ground, the hard hard ground, and old paper and always, all over mice, and they nibble and bite and aren't nearly enough to eat." It broke into a howling.

"Oh, don't cry!" I said, rushing forward. I don't know from whom I'd learned pity—not my family. I fell to my knees beside the wall, my hands against the cold metal. "Is it you, Chris?"

"Chris?" said the voice. "Bad Chris, mad Chris. He's far away, he is long gone, he is a monster, isn't he, T-Tina? Yes he is, Mother. But Old Dave came to teach us a lesson, so Chris has gone to market to buy a bird skin to wrap his big brother in."

"Dave?" said Gary. Trish shrugged. It was a common name in Inglewell, but I didn't know an Old Dave.

"Mitch," I said gently. "Listen."

"Monster," said the voice, contrite. "No Mitch, all monster. Only T-Tina wasn't a monster, wasn't she? Yes, Mother. You were clever."

My skin crawled. *Monsters.* Yet my mother had spoken harshly about Gary and Trish, too, and here they were, helping. And this was my brother.

"Why was I clever?" I asked patiently. Gary and Trish had found another door beyond a row of shelving lined with tins; Gary had put the hammer down and was picking the lock.

"It was your idea, you got to stay, little piggy stayed home. The ground is so hard, T-Tina."

"Hurry," I said to Gary. My eyes stung.

Trish shook her head. "I'm not *comfortable* with this."

"It's Mitch!" I shouted. Gary grunted in agreement, or surprise.

"Maybe he's locked in for a reason," said Trish. "Let's get my dad. After all this time, another hour or two won't hurt."

This is how the world can be made to work, my dad had said.

I steadied my breath. "Patricia," I said, carefully. "You do want to help, don't you?"

Trish paused, frowned. "Of course I do."

Gary cleared his throat. "I'm on your side, Bettina," he said, "but don't try telling us what we want. Or what we are. That's your mother talking."

I opened my mouth to say my mother only ever *asked,* and to be like her was hardly an insult. But truth was shifting the way the land had when we drove: trees sliding behind trees.

"This is hardly time to discuss manners," snapped Trish.

On the other side of the wall Mitch keened—a descending wail that sank into a low sob. Goosebumps ran down my back and arms.

I stood up, brushing dirt off my knees. They were filthy from kneeling on the floor.

"I'm going," said Trish.

Let them go, my mother had said. *They're not worth your worry. You're happy to be with me, without them. Aren't you, Bettina?* But that felt long ago. I had not been this far from my mother since my father left. Gary and Trish were *mine*.

"You—" I began, and saw the set of Gary's shoulders. *My friends.* So I just said, "Please."

Trish pulled her hair.

"Go if you want to," I said. "I'm not leaving him."

I didn't know where *this* key was, but I found a rusted adze propped up against the galvanised iron wall. The splintered haft was solid enough, and the head looked dangerous. I took off my thin cardigan, although the air was dry and stagnant on my bare shoulders, and wrapped it around the handle.

"Please stand aside, Gary Damson," I said, and swung. I missed the lock and punched a ragged tear in the door. The second swing connected.

Trish gave a startled whoop.

The third blow broke the lock. I shook my numbed hands and pulled my cardigan hastily back on. Gary pulled the broken metal loose and pushed the door open.

He felt the wall inside the doorway. "Is there a light here?" he asked. But this room was new to me.

"There's a torch in the glovebox," said Trish. But after she went to fetch it, Gary found a switch and pulled it down with a loud *thunk*. Another bare bulb glowed into life, fading and brightening with the fluctuations of the generator.

In front of us was a concrete-floored corridor walled with piled cages, various sizes, of mesh and chicken wire. The concrete floor was cracked, dirt thick in the ridges left when it was laid.

At the bottom of the first cages were small, limp bundles; the air smelled feathery, over a sweet, desiccated odour of decay. Further back, where the unsteady light cast shifting shadows, birds rustled untidy feathers, crooning protest. I saw dishevelled magpies, a white-eyed crow and, in a despondent huddle, a family of a dozen dirty-grey chatterjacks. Behind them a wedge-tailed eagle sagged, black-bronze feathers tarnished. Such bright beauty, diminished and contained.

"Mitch?" I whispered. At the far end, wire rattled. Gary turned down a path between the cages and we saw.

A wall of heavy weldmesh made a separate enclosure of half the room. The mesh door fit its frame badly but was latched and padlocked. Chicken wire had covered the mesh, once, but now was rusted and frayed. Mitch crouched on the filthy concrete inside.

I couldn't blame anyone who had known him for not recognising my brother. Mitch was gaunt, with matted hair and a beard I'd never seen him wear. His eyes were hollow, smudged. His bones jutted, the old awkwardness of his frame revealed. His long bare toes were clenched and he held a strip of hessian sacking around his narrow shoulders. It was stained dark and shiny. Our shadows fell on him and he smiled, lips pulling away from yellow teeth.

"You look like a ghost," he said pleasantly. "Sitting in the lemon tree."

Puzzled, I glanced at my skirt, my hands. I was dusty with travel, and my clothes were creased, but it was Mitch who appeared less than alive. I glanced at Gary, but he only said, "I've got cutters in the truck. Better than an adze for this door." He turned back. I took his place by the wire.

"Mitch!" I said. "Mitchell, what's happened? Why are you in there?"

"I wouldn't stay when he said *sit*," sighed Mitch. His sunken eyes were bright. "I never could, even if it's for my own good. *Our* own good."

Perhaps he had a fever. Or perhaps he had been sleeping— my mother was distant when she woke, as if still returning from far away.

I crouched down to Mitch's level, holding the mesh. He touched my knuckles. His own were knobbled and dirty, his fingernails black. "We'll get you out," I said. Mitch pinched my fingers as if he was making sure they really were flesh and bone. "Gary will open this and I'll take you home, Mitch— Ow!"

I wrenched my hand away and stumbled backwards. "You bit me!" His teeth had broken skin, and dark blood welled up, but for a moment shock warded off pain. An old emotion stirred: the urge to slap my brother across the ear.

"You can't get me out," said Mitch, dreamily, and added in a childish singsong, "We've been trying for years, yes we have, to get us out. Look."

He shuffled around, letting the hessian fall. I forgot my own hurt. The back of his shirt was cut away. Dirty dressings, peeling from his pale skin, revealed long, red-edged seeping wounds. No wonder he wasn't well.

Mitch shrugged the covering up again and turned, lifting his arms to show cuts at his wrist and underneath, from armpits to elbow. They were ragged, untended, but looked deliberate. I couldn't imagine the purpose. Through all the scents of that room, I caught a putrid sweetness, somehow familiar.

"Nothing takes," said Mitch, gently resigned. His face was sallow, and the thin skin of his eyelids hooded his gaze. It made him look like the languishing eagle. "All these birds. I liked catching them. They laugh at us, but then they die. They don't help."

"Don't help what?"

"Old Dave says it will take this time, next time, it must. We have Dad's papers. But it won't, because it isn't maths, it's . . ." He frowned at the ceiling, head tilted to one side. "It's law. *She* didn't say we could stop being monsters, ever. But we'll try; we've got help. I said you'd help us. That was my idea. Chris made me stop painting, but I was right, wasn't I?"

I couldn't answer. I'd grown so used to my mother's relentless reasonableness.

His attention strayed. "So few feathers . . ."

I wrapped the hem of my cardigan awkwardly around my hand and thought about infection and Mitch's yellow teeth.

"I don't understand," I said. "What are you trying to do? Dave who? Where is Chris?" There was a cold particularity to how the cuts followed the lines of his shoulder blades, his arms. "Who did this to you?"

Mitch, startled, ducked his head and whined, "*You* said we were monsters."

"I never did!"

"It wouldn't have taken otherwise," said a man's voice behind me. Not Gary's. "Mum wasn't that convincing. Not alone."

I scrambled to my feet, turning, and saw the stranger from outside the petrol station: tall, with overgrown sandy hair, but far too young to be our father. He looked at my white sandals, my sundress, my hair, and through his ragged beard I saw his lip curl. "She did a number on you, though, Tink," he said.

It was Chris.

He was grease-stained, lean and sunburned, with bones sharp at his cheeks and wrists. All the boyishness of him had gone, and the laughter in his eyes wasn't pleasant, but for a moment, I believed everything might be all right.

I darted forward, flung my arms around his ribs and felt a stinging in my throat, my eyes. *We won't waste tears on them, will we, Bettina?* But he smelled of engine oil, blood, sweat and memory.

"Knock it off, Tink," said my brother, ungently. He prised me away and held me at arm's length, but I was too happy to mind.

"Have you been here all along?" I asked. "Why didn't you come home, or call? Is— Is Dad here? What's wrong with Mitch?" My back was to the mesh; Mitch's fingers poked at my ankle through the wires.

"Mitch," said Chris, glaring at our elder brother, "kept trying to get out. So I locked him in. He thought you might be useful. I told him we weren't wanted in Runagate."

"I wanted you!" I said. Again that snap as if a thread had broken deep in my chest. I wiped my eyes with the heels of my hands. *We don't want them, do we?* "You're my brothers! You aren't"—I gestured around—"*this*. Come home, Chris. Someone should look after you."

"You?" scoffed Chris. "You're no better than Dad, Tink. Playing games with people's lives." He narrowed his eyes. "But you aren't playing."

"Of course I'm not!" I snapped. It felt good. I hadn't fought with my brothers for too long. Chris let go of my shoulders and turned my face roughly up. He was tall.

"You aren't even *Tink* anymore," he said, and let go, rubbing his hands as if I were the dirty one. His fingernails were black crescents. "You're just a shell. Well, Nerida might have got Dad and you, but she's not getting us."

"She only *has* me." Then I realised they might not know what had happened, or that people thought Dad was dead. "Chris, Dad never came home."

I would have gone on, told him what Gary told me, but Chris snorted. "He never left."

"What lovely, lovely lemons," murmured Mitch feverishly, near the floor. The birds around us were quiet. "What fine fruit, Mrs Scott; how do you grow them in this soil? Blood and bone, blood and bone." He laughed and pinched the tendon at the back of my ankle. I jumped forward.

"Stop it, Mitch!" I said. "Chris—"

"Do you know Mr Alleman drives to Woodwild and talks to the trees?" Mitch whispered.

I tried not to think of Gwenda's story—the Woodwild school was nothing to me; I had found my brothers. Yet if there was any truth to Gwenda's story, our father was there when Jim Alleman and the other children vanished. I shook off the thought.

"Dad went away!" I insisted. "He'd always been *emotionally absent* . . ." I trailed off. Those words came from my mother's books, and she'd only read those after she'd persuaded my father to move us to town. That it would be easier to raise a daughter there.

I remembered. I had visited this place with my father, yes, but once, we'd all lived in that house, near this shed, the boys shouting and the dust like a golden veil in the sunlight—how could my fastidious mother have endured the roughness of it, the unconstrained light and limbs?

"He left us." But this certainty was fracturing.

What did I know for sure? Dad's car was found crashed. Trish's dad had come to Upper Spicer Street. My mother had been shocked, gentle. *We don't need to dwell on that, do we, Bettina? We were here all night. Bettina was here with me, weren't you, Bettina?* But Gary and Trish were sure I'd been with them.

No, that was wrong. They said they'd *covered* for me.

"People pitied Nerida," said Chris, amused. I wished he'd say *Mum*—he sounded so superior. "Do you really think Aberdeen asked her any hard questions? Do you think anyone would look where she didn't want them to? Digging up her garden?"

"Why would they?" I retorted. "They found a car, not a body."

"Exactly," said Chris.

Mitch was humming a high, wretched little song.

"There's some interesting family history in those boxes," said Chris, nodding past the cages to the closed door. "Ever wonder how someone like Dad got a wife like her? She isn't *our* mother, you know. We came along first, Mitch and I. And one day: there was Nerida Scott. So pretty, so quiet. A perfect lady." Chris sneered again. "She stole his heart." He cocked his head, birdlike and unblinking. "But he offered it up. I thought *you* might have fought harder. I suppose, technically, you were already her creature. She certainly made quick work of you."

He coolly flipped away the hair on one side of my neck, then the other, as if expecting to find a mark. Frowning, he pointed down to the cardigan, its hem wound around my hand.

"Mitch bit me," I said. The throbbing had eased, and I unwrapped the cloth. "It will be fine, but I suppose I ought—" The bloody marks were closing, although the bruises from Gary's fingers remained. He should have been back. "It's Mitch I'm worried about. Let's—"

"Shh," said Chris.

"I've been quiet long enough!" I snapped, startling myself. "I've agreed with everyone else long enough, and now—"

Chris laughed. "Was it that simple? She'd already turned you into a real little yes-man, before we left. You'd agree to anything she said. *Poor Mum.* Oh, Tink. So much for having a mind of your own. She didn't have to eat your heart—you gave it to her. She gets a slave and all the power you had from Dad, and you sleepwalk into our arms."

"Power?" I said. I didn't want to think about eating hearts—or the sweet, familiar smell of rot. "She gardens and cooks and writes letters. Mitch is *sick*, Chris—"

"A perfect life," said Chris, over me. "But we've got you now."

Chris must be sick too. Trish and Gary could help me persuade him—where *were* they?

"Mum knows I'm here," I lied.

"Of course she does," said Chris, soothingly. "I heard it over the two-way, driving back. Someone asking if anyone had seen a Damson Fencing truck, last headed this way—with you in it. Sounded like Nerida's policeman. Imagine my surprise! Nerida's bold, if she lets the Damsons hang around you. They were always suspicious about Dad's . . . interests."

From beyond the thick walls of this room, through the crowded cavern of the shed, over the steady thrumming of the generator, came a sound like a slammed truck door.

"Chris," whined Mitch.

Chris shook his head. "Old Dave will deal with it." He returned his attention to me. "Though I'm surprised Gary Damson cared for your company—he was getting over-certain about how the world should work. I wouldn't think you'd have fit his family's tidy view of things. As for you, sis— I'm beginning to think Mitch might have a point."

"Thank you, thank you very much," muttered Mitch. I was glad of the interruption. Fever and infection could be dealt with.

"We have to get him to hospital."

But Chris kept talking to Mitch—or himself. "She might have what we need, after all. We're missing something— Dad's touch, as it were. And if it worked for Nerida . . ." He nodded judiciously. "Nothing to be lost by finding out."

"What—" I began, but Mitch had stood up behind me, and his fingers grasped my throat through the mesh.

I grabbed his hand, but his bony fingers were strong. "Nothing personal, Tink," he said in my ear. I struggled for breath, kicked and tried to drop free, but Mitch's grip only tightened. "Mitch!" I choked. "Chris!" The light flickered.

Chris moved as if he were underwater. From of the leather holder on his belt he took a pocket knife. He unfolded the longest blade, turned it casually so it flashed through the gathering dimness. I still thought he would save me.

"Unless Mitch has any more bright ideas," he said calmly, through the thunder of blood in my ears, "I'm sorry if I don't get this right first time. I've never actually gone for the heart before."

THE RETURN

Trish never asked to be in a story, never believed them. That would tie her to all the injustices and angers of her father's family, to the great absence of her mother.

She spent her childhood closing her eyes to the tawny-grey ghost that smoked through the bush when she went outside of Runagate. Something not a dingo, not a feral dog, trailing her through the trees. She'd ignored it, explained it away, although it glimmered through her dreams until she'd tattooed it on her shoulder in . . . defiance, she supposed.

She almost convinced herself it wasn't her fault that, with her return from university, the impossible creature began to be seen again in Old Pinnicke's haunts. Later, she would say she hallucinated everything. There wasn't any evidence, after all.

Trish went to Gary's truck to fetch the torch. She stood a moment under the molten sky, breathing. Inglewell was both too small and too large. In the city, nothing tried to prise open her skull, her ribs until she believed in curses and miracles, witches and vengeance.

She lit a cigarette to settle her mind, and almost welcomed the buzzing of an engine, the orange plume of dust behind a ute thumping down the rutted road from the gate. Then she realised what it meant. She ran a few steps, went back for the shotgun and walked around the other side of the building, through the scrap heap, out of sight of the approaching vehicle.

She didn't see Gary leave the shed.

Something, she said, the one time she talked about it, flicking the lighter so the flame spurted briefly. It was sunset, and *something* found her. The worst was, for a moment she was glad. She heard an unutterable wail from the distant bush, like a warning, and for an instant, primed by the long day, hungry, anxious, she *wanted* to see the dog-wolf-thing.

But *something* shifted between rusted tin and abandoned tyres, elbowing into the red light. Too many elbows. It was bony and gelatinous at once, a thing, a *person* that had been taken apart and put together wrong, that was trying to be too many creatures at once. But it could speak.

"Blood calls to blood," it said. "In I come to see my friends, my boys, my *apprentices,* and find *you.* I remember *you.* You stole my life, girl. Twice over."

David Spicer, or whatever he had become, had once been like Darryl Scott. He had believed in stories. He had believed in talking his way into and out of difficulties, surviving in mockery of everything that should have destroyed him. But at some point, everyone's story gets taken out of their hands. It happened three times to David.

First was the woman who had—no one is left who knows how—traded him a wild twilight existence for his youth. Then her daughter, Linda, who seized his freedom and dragged him back into humanity and old age. And then there was her granddaughter.

Trish fired.

Her dad had taught her. She was a good shot.

When she came back into the shed, her hands on the shotgun were steady.

CHAPTER SEVEN

A TRUE HISTORY OF BLOOD AND FIRE

Don't remember this: the heft of a body, fully human, so much weightier than bird-boys and flower-women. Forget rending steel, the car where it slumped. Don't remember where you dropped the keys (maybe they've been found, added to a rattling graveyard of metal). Don't remember limping home through the trees, believing them empty.

They were always full of ghosts.

You were already becoming one.

Darkness, and a rolling thunder like the end of the world.

My legs felt heavy. I sprawled on the floor, against Mitch's cage. Above me, Trish stood holding the shotgun. I smelled blood, the scorched-iron-and-earth of gunpowder. Her knuckles were pale.

Chris had fallen across my legs, his back and side a sticky mess. He moved his hand, but I grabbed the knife.

Trish ejected the shell calmly. It rolled with another on the floor. She tried to put down the shotgun, but it slipped from her hand and fell, ringing on the concrete. "Oh, shit," she said, distantly. She was bloodied, too. A fine mist. "Oh, shit. Gary. *Chris.*"

"What happened?" Gary said from the doorway. He was holding a wadded-up rag to his head, and looked like he was going to throw up, but he was carrying the bolt cutters.

My throat and my head were burning; my ears rang.

"Tell me they're alive," mouthed Trish.

I dragged my feet from under Chris. He was too easy to move. Light.

"Tina?" said Gary, thinly. He reached my side and turned my face toward him. "Are you okay? Can you hear me?"

"I'm well, thank you," I said. I shook my head to clear my ears. Gary let go, picked up the shotgun and turned to Trish. Sitting, I put the knife carefully into the pocket of my dress. It scraped the note I should have shown my mother. None of this would have happened.

"Don't faint, either of you, or I'll go too," said Gary, more distinctly. He kept wincing, but with me out of the way, he cut the lock, put his shoulder to the gate and pushed it open, moving Mitch with it. Once he was inside, he bent unsteadily and touched Mitch's neck. This wasn't Gary's job. Nor Trish's. This was *my* family.

"They're alive," he said, but Trish, looking at the blood welling from the holes in Chris's shirt, didn't see Gary's face.

"First aid," I said, clearing my throat. "Help me, Gary."

We dragged Chris from the narrow corridor of cages into Mitch's large pen. I pulled off my cardigan and held it against his worst wounds. Blood quickly soaked it. I tried not to look at Mitch.

"He wouldn't let go of her," Trish said. "I had to shoot them both. Mitch wouldn't let go." She kept saying it.

Chris's face was an awful colour. When he opened his mouth, his teeth were stained with blood; it trickled into his beard.

"He said Sergeant Aberdeen was looking for us," I told Gary.

"Hear that, Trish?" said Gary, not heartily. "Your dad's on his way. It'll be okay." But he stumbled as he picked up a length of dirty sacking. He put it under Chris's head. Gary had been friends with my brothers, too, I remembered, although Mrs Damson hadn't approved. We'd rattled around together. *We.*

Trish wrapped her arms around herself. She was shivering.

"You'll be fine," I said to Chris, and almost believed it. Not enough.

"You can't fix everything with talking," Chris said. "Even Old Dave couldn't make it *right*."

I looked at Gary, his freckles dark against his skin. "Who?" he mouthed.

I didn't know. I didn't want to hear about strangers.

"Said he'd fix us." Chris coughed—a mockery of a laugh. "Guess you got in first, Tink. Fixed us good." I could hardly protest. Between us, we'd killed him. Nearly. "Well," Chris finished, his voice bubbling in his throat, "winner takes all."

"That's not true," I said. "If you two die, what do I have left?" I had my mother, the empty perfection of the yard in Runagate, set apart forever from the crawling loveliness, the burnt-velvet bush of Inglewell. Gary and Trish were shocked and silent—perhaps I had lost them, too.

"No monsters is . . . hardly a loss," Chris managed.

"You're no more monsters than I am." I needed to keep him talking. "Tell me what else you are." No answer. "Chris!"

"Boys," he said. His mouth was an awful colour. "Brothers. Sons."

"And before that?"

His eyes were dull. "You're hers, Tink. That's why she keeps you. We were *his*—she could never own us that way. But Dad still liked you better than us. We were monsters."

"Terrors, yes," I conceded. "But so was Gary. You were boys like any others, after all. Weren't you?"

"I was too heavy," he said. "We never broke bones, falling. Remember? I used to dream of flying."

Gary hovered over Trish, who crouched on the concrete, her eyes closed, swearing in a long whisper. I only caught "—I wanted to be a *teacher*, not a murderer." The living birds shrieked and rasped.

Chris clawed at his throat, his chest. "We tried to get out," he said. "His mistake was making us too heavy." The sketches of wings in the shed, the cuts along Mitch's arms . . . had they tried to graft *feathers* to him? "But they won," Chris said. "Dad made us into boys, and you and Nerida turned us into monsters, and that's how they'll bury us. Bone's a heavy cage, Tink. Even Old Dave couldn't—shouldn't have . . . trusted him."

"You were meant to be birds," I said, ruffling his feathered hair. He would never have let me, once. *Feel something,*

I thought, but all I could think of was the cold pressure of filthy concrete under my knees; the reek of birds and blood; the terrible ruin of two boys who had tried to take themselves apart into whatever they believed our father had made them from. The flickering light made Chris's expression shift and twist.

"You were an accident," he said. "You shouldn't have existed, and they both loved you best." His voice bitter and strained, he said abruptly, "Why should you be treated better than us? I'm *glad* she got to you, made you into what someone else wanted you to be." But he let me hold his hand. "You're more her than you," he whispered.

"No," I said. "I'm me. I'm Bettina Scott and I—I won't be told what to do."

Behind me, Gary talked urgently to Trish. I heard him say, "Self-defence. Or defence, anyway. It'll be okay, Trish."

It wouldn't. Not if we went on like this, huddled in this filthy shed. I had seen so much sky, all day.

I put one hand on Chris's forehead and stretched to brush the other against Mitch. He didn't stir, but where my fingers touched his neck I felt the thready jump of a pulse.

I had no idea what I was doing. Even my mother, who knew things, couldn't have known how to do this. She'd have done it long before, otherwise. *Beaks and claws, that's what little boys are made of.*

I could almost hear her. *You're in shock, Bettina. You need to rest, and settle your imagination. No excitement. That's what you need, isn't it?*

"You were born to be birds," I said. Chris sighed. Mitch didn't make a sound. Gary watched me while he talked to Trish, but I couldn't read his face. Damsons, everyone said, didn't approve of Scotts.

"I don't know what sort of birds," I went on. "There isn't

time for me to find out; I don't think I can talk you into living much longer as you are. But in your bones you must know. I'm counting on you. You're going to be brave again, aren't you?"

"You probably don't need to force them to agree," said Gary wearily. "I'm starting to think—as far as I can tell—it's your saying it that's important."

I would ask later how Gary guessed, why he wasn't surprised by what I was doing, why exactly Damsons looked askance at Scotts. For now, I whispered to my brothers. "You *are* brave. You're wild. You *need* to be. It's not monstrous. It's because you were meant to be birds."

Both Mitch and Chris were motionless.

Far as we had come from home today, we were still within Inglewell. The web of Runagate, Woodwild, Carter's Crossing. The circle of my father's laughter and my mother's words. Whatever my brothers ought to be, whatever I was, we were trapped by our history. I bit my lip, gathered all my will, the thorny memories I'd been given or had forced upon me. I had my father's blood but his heart as well, and something of my mother, surely: the catechism of spoken power that had hidden my past—that, more, had healed my arm where it had been scratched, and bruised, and broken. Under my collarbone a tendril snapped, like heartbreak.

"Be birds," I whispered. "Be birds."

I held my breath as long as I could, shut my eyes. When I breathed out, I heard a shifting: a long rustling, a beating of wings that stirred my hair and clattered past—broad harsh feathers, trailing silken ones, pinions that whistled in the air and down that fell softly on my hands. I sat on the floor of the shed, eyes closed, until there was silence.

THE GETTING
OF WISDOM

These stories of Inglewell, like the tellers, are hybrids of tales from distant woods and forests. I cannot believe our silky oaks, our ironbarks, the shimmering brigalow are less handsome than those fabled groves, but the stories (even those, like us, half-made here) fit them uneasily.

Once, somewhere between the Coral Sea and the Indian Ocean, a man went wandering. Men do: men with histories to lose, and others who want to find them, digging a little deeper into the earth, looking a little more keenly over their shoulders.

A few passed their knowledge on as a warning; some kept moving ahead of the stories that tracked them, or—like the Damsons—set up boundaries: rules and fences.

Others had easier consciences.

This particular man found his way to Inglewell: Carter's Crossing, Runagate, Woodwild.

He was unburdened by everything except desire. He wanted what most people want, good or bad: an easy life; a quiet life; occupation of his choice; to live forever or, if that could not be managed, to leave a mark to say he had stood upon the earth, over all who went before.

Doubtless he followed rumours of knowledge: curses and blood, things fenced out (or in). He played on Woodwild's fears, walked paddocks and hills and scrub until he found mysteries to amuse him, stories towed bedraggled from other lands, lessons unlearned, a scraping of secrets glittering like gold-dust.

He picked up things kicked over in the dirt. He flipped through old books, borrowed advice from others like him. He was determined to seize what he could of the world for himself. He dismantled bright wild things, added to them, forgot them—forgot, too, that men can be taken apart as easily. Once the soul of a man is removed, it can't be put back again.

At last, he settled in a hidden corner of Inglewell and made himself sons. He was unpracticed, but birds and bones, blood and fire can make something like enough to two wild boys. Always climbing, jumping, shouting for the sky.

Having learned that two wild boys are a life's endeavour, he tested his skills again and made a wife to care for the boys, and him. She was beautiful, fair as flowers, uncomplaining. She had no choice: flowers are rarely vocal in their objections.

Life went well. Oh, there were dangers. His was far from the only story hidden in the trees. Some he could not see. A few (a scaly burnt whisperer with yellow eyes, always hungry, always diminishing) followed him for their own reasons. From some he learned all he could and, when they weakened, put them away. A shovel and the trees can conceal a great deal.

Then his wife bore a child—his third, her first. A daughter. His own flesh and blood, with the same furious curiosity, the burgeoning power that had driven him to understand what ought to have stayed hidden. The bird-boys were proof of his abilities; the girl would continue them. His confidence grew. He moved his family into town at his wife's quiet desire and to gratify his own pride, but continued his researches. Into what, I could not say. He found money.

His wife, brought unwillingly into a world of rough and dissonant voices, made her own plans.

Even flower women grow and change, with the strange alchemy of time and childbirth; they talk among themselves (did you think she was the only such woman in the world?). One night, when even the yielding flesh of flowers could bear no more, when the children were on the edge of flying away and the little strength she drew from them, the mild authority she exercised, would be lost to her, she strangled her husband, easily as a vine, buried him in the pits he'd dug for her fruit trees, and planted the saplings over him.

The girl was hers and the girl's strength of mind could be turned to her service. The boys—clashing and heartless— she banished as monsters. They fled, trapped in a form never truly theirs, always trying to turn back into birds.

There were books and letters to teach her how to be real, to be a lady, although one who wilted in the heat of afternoon, who drew life from the lemons that drank her dead husband's strength.

How gracious and peaceful life was.

CHAPTER EIGHT

ALL SUNS SET

When I opened my eyes, the cages had been emptied of dead and living birds, and I was quite alone. I stood, aching from the chill of the concrete, my dress stiff with drying blood.

I abandoned my ruined cardigan—no amount of white vinegar or careful mending would save it—and limped through the shed. The sun was setting, great sheets of scarlet and gold up the bowl of the sky, rubied with smoke from beyond the screen of saplings, and Gary was running water from the jerry can on the back of his truck onto Trish's hands. In that light, I couldn't see if it poured away bloody.

"Trish—" I began, but she pushed away from the truck

and ran to the side of the shed. The wolf tattoo stretched and leapt. I could hear her being sick.

"Give her time," said Gary. He was pale, even in that red light. He'd washed the blood from his spiking hair—I could see where Chris must have hit him when he went to the truck for the cutters. He leaned against the tailgate.

"My mum would have said I shouldn't get involved," he said, as if it were a heavy thought. "That's the point of being a Damson, apparently. You just . . . don't do anything."

"Even for friends?"

"Well," said Gary. He shrugged. I remembered the story he had told us. The wishes.

Dazed with the afternoon's events, I said, "Do you believe you forced us to be your friends? With your—wish?"

He looked guilty, then glanced up at an angle, wistful. "You really remember? Being friends?"

I needed time too, but Trish was sick and Gary didn't look much better. "Mostly, I remember being annoyed at you," I said sturdily.

I knew I should *make* Trish be well. The boys had been beyond my power, but this, even if she didn't thank me, was the correct thing to do. I could tell her she would be better, she hadn't done anything wrong, everything was all okay. And it might be. For a while. Then one day she would feel an ache, a fear.

I leaned cautiously back, not too close to Gary. I was tired: a new bone-weariness all my own, every piece of me present and heavy as lead.

"How are you feeling?" I asked Gary, carefully phrasing it as a question. He didn't reply. Glancing across, I saw him smile tightly and shake his head.

"Here comes the cavalry," he said.

The police car grumbled down the track, its dust-cloud pale against the growing dusk. It rounded the house and came through the trees.

"This won't be simple," Gary added. We walked to meet them.

Sergeant Aberdeen got out. My mother emerged from the passenger side. She was beautiful, moth-pale in the evening.

"My poor Bettina!" She held her hands toward me, but when I reached her, she stepped back. She looked thinner, almost translucent. "Bettina!" she cried. "What have you been doing?"

I looked down. My dress was covered with dust and oily dirt, torn by wire, spattered with my brothers' blood. Blood had dried sticky on my hands and arms, and a wetter stain stuck the bodice of my dress to my skin. I put my hand to my chest and drew it away with a gasp. Chris had cut me after all, before—before.

"It will be fine," I said, faintly. "I'll be fine." It hurt less, I thought. I could believe it was healing.

"What have they done to you?" said my mother. "It was that Damson boy, wasn't it?" She wouldn't blame Trish, not with the sergeant standing there. "He isn't a good influence—I told you, didn't I, Bettina?"

I wanted to say, "Yes, Mother." I'd spent three years telling myself I was a good girl. We would return to our peaceful life, and she would teach me to believe this was a dream. I would agree and forget.

"No," I said. "I did this."

"You're in shock." My mother touched my forehead quickly, with cool hands. Over everything I smelled lemon flowers. But what were they, or any of the coaxed and tortured plants in our garden? They grew from blood and bone, murder and power.

"No," I said. "And I *lied* before. I didn't do this. You did."

She opened her eyes wide, and put a slim hand to her chest. *"I?"* She turned to Sergeant Aberdeen; he was looking past her. Looking for Trish.

"You will help me to convince her to come home, Win," she pleaded. *Win.* I looked at Winston Aberdeen still standing by her. This power was all her own. "You know how . . . fragile she is. This could push her too far. I couldn't bear it. Not again. Not like—" She put her hand over her mouth.

"Like what?" said Sergeant Aberdeen.

"Oh, I haven't proof," said my mother, pressing her hands to her temples, as if in pain. "That horrible night. She was so angry with her father when they left; she was such a wild, strong thing in her rages."

She didn't look at me. Maybe she meant it. I was taller and stronger than her.

He regarded me narrowly. "I was told—Nerida, you said she was with you that evening. You confirmed it, Bettina."

"I wasn't with my dad," I said. Dead, all he knew and understood gone with him. "I'd forgotten. I was out with"—I stumbled, still wanting to say *Patricia*—"Trish and Gary and, and my brothers. Driving. Playing *tag.*"

Such a petty crime. There'd been the fireworks—they'd scorched the tank stand at the school; Trish brought rum. Then we'd driven around Runagate with the headlights off, looking for each other in the dark. *I'd* driven. I looked at my hands. Odd to imagine them on a steering wheel.

Hurt and betrayal twisted my mother's fine features. She hadn't doubted me, I realised. I'd lied so easily. I'd crashed Dad's car, limped, sore and guilty, back to town and climbed in the window, although it hurt. She hadn't known, hadn't noticed my stiffness, had been too distracted to notice the small cut on my cheek, easily hidden by hair. Or perhaps she had noticed, and thought I'd been fighting my brothers. She'd made me agree that I'd been in all night—I'd been willing, afraid what would happen when they learned I'd written off the car—and help her. *Help* her! The smell of incense and raw meat in the house . . . I wondered, distantly, what manner of advice she had received in those letters with their mysterious stamps. The sap of lemons welcome on my hand when I went to help her plant the new trees in the garden. I'd been so eager to forget.

Standing with the cold dirt of the track silting into my shoes, I took Chris's knife out of my pocket. The blade was dull under the apricot sky, crusted with blood—mine and Chris's.

"Now—" began Sergeant Aberdeen.

"Do you recognise this?" I asked my mother. "Dad never went anywhere without it." The scratching on the red plastic casing—*D S*, the D flat-bottomed, as if altered from another letter—was worn almost smooth against my palm.

"Where did you find it?" Panic unfurled in her eyes. "You found it here? Winston." She turned to Sergeant Aberdeen as if he were the sun. "Could Darryl have come this way?"

"Chris had it," I said. I touched my ruined neckline. The seeping cut that began at my collarbone was not, perhaps, so deep as I'd thought. "He tried to cut my heart out."

I saw realisation in her eyes and added, "I wonder where he got that idea."

"Gary Damson," said Sergeant Aberdeen. "Can you cast any light on this?"

"Family matters, sir," said Gary, rallying a note of respectful insolence. "You know Damsons don't get involved."

"I crashed Dad's car that night," I said to Sergeant Aberdeen. "I walked back into town and climbed in the window." *Bruises spilling hydrangea-blue across my chest and stomach.*

"However my dad left, Sergeant Aberdeen, he didn't drive. And my brothers have been living here. We frightened them and"—I looked hard at Trish's father, telling him the truth so he would believe it—"Chris and Mitch have gone."

"Their ute is here," said Sergeant Aberdeen, gesturing toward the house.

"Then wherever they went," I said, firmly, "they didn't drive."

"Bettina," said my mother, her gentle voice strained. "Sergeant Aberdeen can ask you about this tomorrow, can't he? You're excitable. Come home where everything is pretty and neat, and tidy yourself up, and all will be well, won't it?"

Don't answer that. "You killed my father," I said. Nothing felt real in this lilac dimness, sweet with dust and rank with smoke, between the shed and our old house. Nothing except me. In this light, I convinced myself I could speak without consequences. "You buried him under the lemon tree and— maybe you ate his heart, I don't know, but whatever you got out of that, it wasn't enough to save yourself. Not without my help, telling you you're beautiful and loved and strong, over and over, so it would stay true. I won't give you that this time."

"Then I will take it," she said. She sprang; I did not step aside. Her fine, sharp fingers clung and tore at the cut on my chest.

I'd been holding the knife, still open.

I remember the scent, the weight of flowers. And then only air.

THE PATHS BY WHICH WE REACH THE WORLD

Rose, lemon, lily, rosella. Lace and etiquette, tea and honey.

Nothing of Nerida Scott, nothing she loved, was from Runagate. All came from across one ocean or another. Yet she belonged to Inglewell entirely. She never left. She could not. She'd been planted as surely as the lemon tree on her husband's grave. Tethered as securely as any story left there, as the memories of people vanished between the trees.

Is that a dingo crying in the night, or a child? Is that a bird calling as the light falls? Are those the bones of a horse glinting white in the paddock? Is that the body of a woman, or merely falling flowers?

The schoolchildren of Woodwild, David Spicer, Linda Aberdeen, all who went before and alongside and after them: they are trapped by the stories that made them and dragged them in; they are caught and held by town and road and lantern-bush and trees.

CHAPTER NINE

HOME AGAIN

Sergeant Aberdeen took the knife, but what else could he do? There was no other evidence, no one to believe him. He turned the knife over and over, as if he could unwind a secret, until Trish stopped him. "Dad," she said. Gary had given her a jacket from his truck, but she was shivering. "Dad, let's go."

"Trish," said Gary, helplessly.

She looked back. Her mascara had run, and in the harsh headlights, it made her eyes huge. "Gary, I'm fucking *unravelling*," she said. "This whole place—Runagate, *Inglewell*. I can't get away. Just—"

"Tomorrow," I said. "We'll talk in town." Her dad, I

thought, would need her as much as she needed him. At least they had each other.

Sergeant Aberdeen pulled his attention back to us. "Get back to Runagate and stay there," he said, as if he would think of something to ask us. "Are you in any state to drive, Gary Damson?"

We watched the lights of the police car pull away, blinking red between the trees. After a while, I said, "You aren't, though."

"I suppose all this is yours," he said, instead of answering.

Whether my mother never existed on paper, officially, or my father had left everything to me, that was another reason my mother had needed me. My mother, already fraying in my mind to only a fall of flowers, white on the ground.

I looked at the shed, full of secrets. Ours and others'. Possibilities, cut short and waiting. Gary followed my gaze.

"Let's burn it," I said. "All of it."

We dragged a good part of the rubbish—stinking, clattering and yielding—from behind the shed up against its walls, and set it on fire: me with an eye on Gary in case he collapsed. My throat was burning and my scabbing cuts kept breaking open. The house was easier to light.

The night was cold on our backs, on my bare shoulders, but we stayed warm watching to make sure the fires didn't get away. The shed collapsed in foul smoke, and the house folded down off its stilts almost with a sigh. The sparks went up to the stars.

"Don't you wonder what was in there?" Gary said, wistfully, when it was far too late.

"I'm trying not to."

"My family thinks there are three types of people in the world," he said, and counted them off on his fingers. "Ones who can't, or haven't, or don't want to see . . . *things*. The Aberdeens, for instance. Mr Alleman. Two: families who know what's going on—"

"Like the Damsons?"

He shrugged, apologetic. "It's what my gran *says*. We're charged with keeping things on an even keel."

A hint of grandiosity in those words. I said drily, "Charged by whom?"

"Ourselves, I think. And number three: People Who Meddle." With a rueful expression at the smoke rising from my father's notes, my brother's experiments, he added, "I'm afraid if I look, I'll find those last two are sides of the same coin."

"What type am I, Gary Damson?" I asked.

He was silent a while, fading firelight turning his face into a mask. "I don't know," he said at last. Not since we were very young had I heard him sound *lost*.

"Whatever it is," I said, "let's get you home."

"I'm afraid of the dark," I lied as we stopped at the gate, when what I wanted to say was *I killed my mother, Gary.* When he stepped into the ghastly glare of the headlights, I slid into the driver's seat and adjusted it and the mirrors before he returned.

He must have been sick, or didn't want to linger in the whispering grass so near the trees, quarrelling. At any rate, he didn't point out that last time I'd driven a car, I'd crashed it. He wasn't even sarcastic when I struggled with the gears. Harder than remembering how to ride a bicycle. Easier than sitting in the passenger seat, thinking.

We had a long drive back to Runagate, the road bleached in our lights, cold and fright and weariness settling into my fingers where they knotted on the steering wheel. My jaw, set, was stiffening and my neck began to ache, but at least I was not thinking of knives and flowers, only remembering how to be alone in my own body.

A hail of moths stormed the headlights and blew away like blossoms. The stars were a great wheel down the centre of the sky. Indistinct animals bounded across our way, at the border of the shadows. Gary's face was turned to the rushing darkness, as if he expected to see something pacing us.

Home, soon. Safe, with the curtains drawn in the warm, pleasant kitchen. I would bring the chicks inside, I decided. But still only I would be there, and the silence of the lemon tree. When I washed my hair, the sink would fill with blood and wilted petals. Here, I did not feel so alone.

"Will Patricia— Will Trish be well?" I asked when we passed Carter's Crossing.

"She just shot a boy she went out with," said Gary. I hadn't known. "And something else happened, when she was outside . . . I'll ask her more tomorrow. You know," he added, as if it were connected, "I didn't realise the old ute your brothers fixed up was Uncle Davy's. Not until I looked at it again tonight. I wonder where they got it. Uncle Davy . . ."

Old Dave.

Gary rolled down the window to shake his head in the chill blast of air. I wanted him to shut it but was too tired to remember how to ask without making him do it, sideways.

"Sorry," he said, before I could shiver. "I'm trying to keep awake."

He rummaged under the seat, only hissing pain once or twice through his teeth, and dug up an old rug. It smelled of horse and engine oil, wire and dirt. He tucked it around my shoulders, then rested his head against the door until we hit corrugations and I heard his teeth jar, saw the faint reflections on the windscreen blur.

"I'll talk to Trish tomorrow," he said. From the corner of my eye I saw him touching his bruises. "She'll pull through. Her dad's all right. He'll convince himself he didn't see anything unusual, didn't see anything at all, and that Mrs Scott—your mum, I mean—has flown . . . *left* town. She's not the first. We'll be— We'll manage."

"You do this a lot, Gary Damson?" I asked, bracingly, instead of saying *Did you see what I saw? Don't you know what I've done?*

"Just trying to convince myself." I didn't look away from the road, but I heard his smile. "Mum won't mind putting you up. You can stay with us."

"Your mother doesn't like me."

"She didn't like that you were a Scott."

"And now I'm a . . . *thing*?" A motherless, murdering thing.

"You're not," he said, with slightly foggy earnestness. "That's real blood. I'll take you home to clean up—"

Home. I still had responsibilities. I had to feed the chooks. Clean the house. Let Mr Alleman, watching over his hedge of lantern-bush, think I was ignorant of our shared histories. Pretend—just until dawn—that everything was as I once believed it to be, before I woke to the whispering blue lace of tree shadows, the awareness of the greater world of Inglewell beyond.

Closer to Runagate, we began to glimpse the lights of farmhouses through the trees. Were the people in them living quiet, inoffensive lives, or did everyone in Inglewell have a secret? People other than us, afraid they weren't entirely human, that a chamber of their heart opened onto caverns. Or sky.

I drove past the petrol station, its sign dim; past the grocery store, dark; the postmaster's night garden. I pulled into Upper Spicer Street and stopped at our house. My house. My mother had left the lights on; moths beat at the windows, but she would never come home to see them.

"She got rid of so many of my dad's things," I said. "We had a fire then, too. What if I never understand everything that's happened, or what to do next?"

"You'll work it out," said Gary. "I mean, presumably your dad learned from scratch. I guess he's not the best example. But you understand. You'll work out what you need to know."

"I know Trish is in shock," I said, struggling with the door handle. I slid down to stand in the driveway. Everything hurt. "And I know you got knocked out, so maybe you were still dazed when you heard what Chris was saying about my dad and when—when everything else happened. Which means you were still knocked out when Chris told me what my dad did. But you weren't surprised."

With difficulty, Gary climbed into the driver's seat and pulled it forward. "I've picked up a bit here and there. Things happen, people talk. It's wild country. And a small town."

"And the Damsons keep things tidy and never liked the Scotts." I closed the door on him. *Gary, my mother is vanishing and I don't know what I am.*

"Bettina," said Gary.

I looked at him.

"You're pretty messed up," he began.

Below everything was that faint strain of friendly fury he had always inspired in me. "Thank you," I answered crisply.

"Tina," he said.

I sighed. His face was too white in the thin glow from dashboard and the kitchen windows. "Gary?"

"Sleep well," he said. "Don't go . . . digging things up, okay?"

"I won't." I was afraid there wouldn't be anything to find. "Drive safely."

"I'll be just down the road," said Gary.

THE SOUL OF THE BONE HORSE

This is the story Gary got later from Vi Damson, his grandmother, who still lived by the fringes of Woodwild, with few vis-
itors except Old Pinnicke. Nevertheless, she heard a great deal.

Your parents don't think it's nice to talk about these things.
Nice. They build half the boundaries in Inglewell: books or
wire, it's all the same. But they might as well be working with
their eyes shut. So, someone has to tell you.

You've heard of the bone horse? That's what we called it. Keeping pace with a car in the night, or—worse—in the daylight through burned scrub, where the light strikes rust-red, iron-grey, chalk-white from its head and flanks.

It's older than me. Older than your great-grandfather. Something like it got around in my grandmother's time, although her letters make it sound smaller.

Stories try to make sense of a land in lots of ways, especially when they've first got their hands on it. Maybe it started as an explorer's horse. Or there were those camel traders. Likely it just began as a pile of bones, resting. You've seen those heaps glimmering white in the trees, so old but never scattered, never dragged away, never properly decaying because they're still lived in.

People talk about spirits of place, but this is different. It's collected the bits and pieces of everything that's been done, and patched them together, then got up and wandered around, breaking fences in the night. Probably doesn't know what it's looking for.

This is what happened after that business at Woodwild:

David Spicer came back from wherever he'd been all those years while Sylvie Spicer ate her heart out. She took strange fancies. Believe me, I know! I was librarian, and a few books she wanted . . . well, I took care she didn't get them. Some fires don't need fuel. But Davy reappeared, old, and met Darryl Scott. I suppose they recognised their own kind.

They set off to catch the bone horse. Botched it, of course: only caught a part—the ghost, the power of it. Something like a soul. Where the horse scavenged that, I don't know—from a deathbed or graveyard; half Inglewell is built on blood. The bone horse wore it loosely. Once, if you saw it, it used to trail a bit of a shine.

The horse vanished for a while. Down the deep dark places of the earth where things go to die, or nurse their wounds, or wait. Time was, if you stretched yourself out and listened to the ground, you'd hear a rustle like heavy canvas, like a body wrapped in a tarp, turning in its sleep.

Of course, Scott and Spicer quarrelled. Scott kept the stuff. Stored it in an old bottle. Maybe he didn't know what to do with it. Maybe he forgot—he kept himself busy enough. And one day Davy Spicer comes to Runagate, talking up the fortunes you could get for junk in farm sheds. Darryl Scott had moved into Runagate by then, bold as you like, and little Tina Scott says to her mother, "What happened to those things Dad used to collect?"

Probably Scott kept more than one secret in the old sawmill after he moved to town. It wasn't rightly his—to be frank, I don't know what you could have called rightly his. But he'd have liked that it stood on treacherous ground. That's why Spicer sent a boy in: lighter, easier to excuse, and if you'd failed—well, boys get hurt every day. Didn't serve in the end. I'd have rested easier if they'd found Spicer's body, after he crashed that ute.

I thought Scott finished him off. But people like that don't have straightforward minds. Always thinking around at you from the side: pestering a place with lantern-bush just to scope out the land; making a wife instead of running off with Gwenda Alleman, like a reasonable man.

So, this is what I guess—and it's only a guess, mind. Davy Spicer crawled away, dug himself a shallow grave, and set himself the long wait of getting better again. Or he crept down into the dark hollows underground, down where water is. Maybe the horse found him and he made a bargain with it. He'd already been dying, and his kind like to have contingencies. That's why he wanted the bottle. He thought he could save himself with it. Take the bone horse's soul like medicine, and rattle on forever, the way it has.

Then we were quiet for a time, until one day a few fools started waving things around again: hearts and birds and lemon trees and a bottle with the dregs of the bone horse's soul. Under the earth, what was left of Davy Spicer dragged itself through caverns. Its bones were mended with wheel spokes and cattle ribs and rusted iron. Broken glass lodged shining in its skull. It crawled back up to where all that commotion was being made. Scott children setting off the ghosts of birds like smoke signals. Started making *deals* again.

But I suppose he wasn't counting on a policeman's daughter with a shotgun and a grudge.

As for the bone horse . . . I never heard a word against it. It was a marvel in its own way. Leave it be. Let things work themselves out. Lock the bottle and what's left in it away, or bury it, or break it. Damsons haven't stayed in Inglewell this long by getting involved.

But you don't like that, do you?

Well, there's something else you might do. Don't tell your mother. But you might give the bottle to that girl. Not the Scott creature. Aberdeen's daughter.

The bone horse isn't the only mystery around Inglewell. Old Pinnicke stopped by, swearing he almost caught that striped beast he's been hunting. Shot off a paw and picked up a woman's hand, ring and all. He'll get the rest of it soon, if he isn't stopped. I don't know if there's much left of the woman, after all these years. But there might be some virtue left in that bottle, to set things right, or at least to change them. And yes, little Miss Aberdeen will care, I think.

ALL THAT SHALL BE

Nothing is as it was.

How in-woven and eternal the district of Inglewell seemed, with its secrets and legends and hatreds.

The mines, marvellous and terrible as any works of man, have laid the dust and sealed the roads. They have turned out the caverns and graves and secret places of the earth, over-written Upper Spicer Street, Lower Spicer Street, and Pinn-icke Road. Flowers from other regions, grasses from other forests brought in idly by wheels of earth-movers, putting down roots uninvited, to bloom and bob in the gardens of people who never thought they'd leave.

But still, in that cradle made by the vanishing towns, where fences sag ill-kept or still tick with the self-satisfaction of a well-built boundary, shadows flit and whisper through the trees. And such trees they are: bottle and box, paper and iron, thorned and blossomed in the light that moves unutterably between them.

ACKNOWLEDGEMENTS

To my parents, Mark and Mary: I turned some memories of my childhood to terrible purposes in these stories, but it was an enchanted time. To my sisters, Angela and Becky: thank you for your encouragement and support, and any vehicular infelicities are entirely my fault. To our neighbours out west: our life there was indelibly shaped by you all, for good. Also none of the people or events in this book are based on you.

To the Vision Writers' Group of old: you first read the idea that would become the chapter "The School in the Wilderness," and were my doorway into all the literary and illustration community I have today. To Kate Eltham in particular: this is what happened to Woodwild.

To Angela Slatter, Lisa Hannett and Delia Sherman: you all read a very early draft, and convinced me to pursue Bettina's story further. Particular thanks to Angela, who is the midwife of this book, and who has made me the writer I am.

To Kim Wilkins and Lisa O'Connell: your advice on the project made me fall in love with research again, and with the beautiful sublime in Australian gothic books. The works of Joan Lindsay, Rosalie Ham and Shaun Tan taught me I wasn't imagining that it was there. To Pamela Freeman and Jodi McAlister: it was a pleasure to deal with you in the academic as well as creative space. The Commonwealth Government Postgraduate Award and the Cecilie Anne Sloane Postgraduate English

Creative Writing Research Scholarship made the degree and this project possible at all, as did the tolerance of my then employer, the Queensland Department of Transport and Main Roads. To Renee Rogowski: you have superpowers.

To Aimee Smith, Caitlene Cooke and Shayna Naran: you suffered more than friendship should be able to demand, and made the book look good.

To Ellen Datlow, Irene Gallo and Ruoxi Chen: you're an inspiration from afar and up close. It's a thrill to be under your care as an author, as much as it has been to work with you previously as an illustrator. To Christine Foltzer and Jaya Miceli: I love what you did to the cover! You made it look like a real book! To the rest of the Tor.com Publishing team—Lauren Anesta, Mordicai Knode, Amanda Melfi, Lauren Hougen, Greg Collins, Richard Shealy, Kyle Avery, and the rest—it's been a dream.

To Alex Adsett: thank you for *getting it.* To Meg Davis: thank you for wise counsel. To Brooke Bolander, Holly Black, C. S. E. Cooney and Kelly Link, who all knew me first as an illustrator: your professionalism, friendship, support and enthusiasm contributed to this book in many ways.

To Pulp Fiction Books, Avid Reader, Black Milk Coffee, Relove Oxley, The Green Man, The Birdcage and others: you know what you did.

To the cactoblastis moth and the prickly pear: your history remains endlessly thrilling.

To others not listed here: thank you.

Final note:

The Iman, Jagera and Turrbal peoples are the owners of and first storytellers on the country where I have lived and live now.

I have tried to acknowledge the bloody history of Australia, even in this version of Queensland that doesn't quite exist, but there are stories I am still learning, and many that aren't mine to tell. Just a few of the wonderful indigenous authors writing now include Alexis Wright, Ellen van Neerven, Ambelin Kwaymullina, Claire G. Coleman and Kim Scott. I hope you will read their books.